William McInnes is one of Australia's most popular writers, delighting readers with his memoirs *A Man's Got to Have a Hobby* and *That'd Be Right*, his novels *Cricket Kings* and *The Laughing Clowns*, and his insight into Australian life since the 1940s, written with Essential Media and Entertainment, *The Making of Modern Australia*. In 2011, with his wife Sarah Watt he co-wrote *Worse Things Happen at Sea*, which was named the best non-fiction title in the ABIA and the Indie Awards in 2012.

An award-winning actor, William has won two Logies and an AFI Award for Best Actor for his role in the film *Unfinished Sky*. He received critical and public acclaim for his leading role in the film *Look Both Ways*, written and directed by Sarah Watt, and starred in the ABC television series 'The Time of Our Lives' and 'Hello Birdie'. William grew up in Queensland and now lives in Melbourne with his two children.

THE BIRDWATCHER

WILLIAM McINNES

hachette
AUSTRALIA

hachette
AUSTRALIA

First published in Australia and New Zealand in 2013
by Hachette Australia
(an imprint of Hachette Australia Pty Limited)
Level 17, 207 Kent Street, Sydney NSW 2000
www.hachette.com.au

This edition published in 2014

National Library of Australia
Cataloguing-in-Publication data:

McInnes, William.

The birdwatcher / William McInnes.

978 0 7336 3297 6 (pbk.)

Man–woman relationships – Fiction.
Fathers and daughters – Fiction.
Bird watching – Fiction.
Romance fiction.

A823.4

Permission to reproduce 'The Night-Ride' from *Selected Poems* by Kenneth Slessor © P. Slessor
(1944), courtesy HarperCollins Publishers Australia
Permission to reproduce 'Waterfall' from *In Middle Air* by Lauris Edmond © Lauris Edmond and
The Pegasus Press 1975, courtesy Lauris Edmond Literary Estate

Cover and text design by Christabella Designs
Cover and internal illustrations by Emma Kelly
Author photograph © Lorrie Graham
Typeset in Sabon LT Pro by Bookhouse, Sydney
Printed and bound in Australia by McPherson's Printing Group

MIX
Paper from
responsible sources
FSC® C001695

The paper this book is printed on is certified against the
Forest Stewardship Council® Standards. McPherson's Printing
Group holds FSC® chain of custody certification SA-COC-005379.
FSC® promotes environmentally responsible, socially beneficial
and economically viable management of the world's forests.

To Bernadette
from William and Sarah

CHAPTER ONE

A group of strangers pushed together for a short time usually ignore each other. Think of a lift: even a happily chatting couple's conversation trickles to silence in the confines of a shared space.

Most trams are filled with people doing just that: not connecting. Some seem actively to repel it – showing a grumpy face, wearing headphones or focusing intense concentration on a book or magazine or tablet. Others don't necessarily want to connect but do show an interest – staring at someone's outfit, listening to phone conversations, glancing out the window at the terrace houses and shops the tram is passing. Others seem to be more open, even willing their fellow travellers to connect with them in some way – meeting their eyes, offering a small smile, showing recognition of those getting on and off and whether they need a seat. And then there are those people who are neutral and seem to have almost no awareness of where they are or who they're with.

David, a tall Anglo forty-something, hangs onto a strap as he stands on the crowded tram. He scans the carriage and its occupants, noting people's movements and the subtle indications of their intentions. The gentle bend of an elbow by an older woman and her raised shoulder hint at her preparation to stand. She shifts her bag to her left hand so she can pull the stop buzzer.

Sometimes, he thinks, sometimes, the way a person holds themselves really gives you a glimpse of their essence – like the young man with the iPad. David regularly sees him on this tram; always dressed in neat fitted suits, his hair styled and his beard as carefully kept as his clothes. Nearly always on his iPad, his thumb sweeping across the screen from left to right, streaming through whatever it is he usually reads. But today his actions are different. David can see his thumb gently falling across the screen both ways. He's looking at something, yes, but he scrolls to and fro. An image or words? The way the man's head tilts slightly, almost imperceptibly, suggests he's looking at an image, David thinks. A photograph. The young man's hand stays still for a few seconds and then moves back and forth again. Every few minutes he looks away from the screen and sighs, turning to the window, and almost always his left hand comes close to his face, his thumb gently touching a gold band on his ring finger.

Another deep breath. He's upset.

If David cranes his neck and leans forward he'll be able to see the image on the screen. He holds his position, uncomfortably contorted but in an inconspicuous way. Good practice, David thinks.

There's a shuffle of feet as the other passengers hanging onto straps move, like birds perched on a branch, and David sees the image on the iPad screen. It's a photo of the young man and another man, almost as neatly styled as the man holding the iPad, embracing on a beach. Then an arm covers the screen and the neat young man sighs again. The passengers in the aisle revert to their original positions.

David resumes his relaxed stance and gently swings on the tram's strap. I was right, he thinks, the man's upset. Well, I hope something good happens for you today, Neat Beard.

Then a flash as a bird passes by the window. David looks out; a seagull. His eyes dart, his attention drawn away from his fellow passengers. Two ravens sit on a power pole, before one drops swiftly onto a garbage bin below. Imported birds – sparrows and starlings and blackbirds – are everywhere. As the housing density increases, so do the number of feral pigeons.

A nature strip along the tramline has been planted with flowering eucalypts. David stares carefully as he passes. Honeyeaters dive about, raiding the gumnut flowers, and he leans forward to look at them, not noticing his invasion of the seated passenger's space until he actually touches the man's head with his body. David pulls back clumsily.

'I'm sorry.'

The passenger shrugs. 'No worries.'

David explains, 'Honeyeaters.'

The passenger looks back to his book. David hesitates, about to say something else, before being distracted by an Indian myna bird flying past.

The tram approaches its next stop. David lets go of his strap and pulls out a very small notebook with an attached pencil. The tram comes to a standstill with the jolt so many Melburnians don't even notice, but which can easily hurl an unsuspecting tourist to the floor or, perhaps worse, into one or more of the less approachable locals.

As he waits for half-a-dozen people in front of him to get off, David has a last look through the windows and, seeing nothing, writes in his notebook, on a page dated already, *Tram 28*.

Stepping down from the tram, his awareness of other commuters kicks in again. Some people almost leap off, some hang on to the handrail and take it one step at a time, some look around carefully for cars, while others are already mentally elsewhere, darting around in front of the tram to cross the road. One action, same intent, so much variation.

David joins the other city workers on the footpath, taking his usual route. Though long-legged, he walks slowly; a country man's mooch, steady and deliberate. He sees a crested pigeon, four spotted doves, blackbirds, a thrush, some white-naped honeyeaters and a seagull. He watches the seagull as it takes flight from a rubbish bin; lit beautifully by the morning sun, it flies across the cityscape. He slows down even further as he walks through a small park, the lawn dappled as the sunlight filters through the trees and bushes. The grevilleas are in flower; their long droopy sprays of beautiful red spiky blossoms stand out against the blue-green foliage.

David automatically veers off the path and pauses below a tall tree. He looks up and checks on a pair of tawny frogmouths, their nest almost invisible. David smiles, as he does every morning that he sees them. A good day then.

Catching a movement in the grevillea, he turns to see, what it is: honeyeaters? No, too small. Silvereyes? He's never seen them here before. He moves aside to let some people go past him but tries not to unsettle the birds. He watches them flit about. Even though they are only about four metres away, he pulls out a pair of small binoculars and focuses on the birds. Silvereyes. They are definitely silvereyes. Bodies the size of an apricot in shades of green feathering into grey, with sharply rendered white rings around their eyes. David continues to watch them for a while, seeing what they are eating. Insects or seeds? Nectar?

Passers-by glance at him curiously. He's tall, and though not exactly in a suit, he's dressed for work, so his binoculars seem out of place, provoking thoughts of a private detective, a spy, a creep, rather than a birdwatcher. As they walk by he pulls out his notebook and turns to a page marked *30th Aug*, where there is a list of ten or so birds. He notes down the ones he has seen on his way from the tram stop, then writes, *Silvereyes (5). East William St (park).*

David climbs up two flights of stairs and walks into an open-plan office, filled with desks and drafting tables. He heads to his own space and dumps his coat, nodding to Rosie, who is working nearby. She smiles at him.

'Hi, David. There are a few messages for you on your desk.'

David lets his nod be his reply and sits down, turning on his computer. He looks at the screen and after a long moment nothing happens.

Go on, David thinks. Just die.

The computer starts in fits like a fluorescent light then settles to on.

I don't hate my job, he thinks. I don't. I am on the side of good.

'Have a nice weekend?' Rosie puts a pile of envelopes in his tray.

David shakes his head, shrugging. 'So-so.'

'Did you go away?'

'No, I went to the football. We lost.'

Rosie is about to speak but David raises his hand. 'I don't want to talk about it. How was your weekend?'

'Lovely. We saw that new movie on Friday night, Saturday was Stephanie's dance final plus Pete's stepmum's brother's fiftieth, which was actually a hoot, even though I was dreading it.'

David doodles on the paper in front of him: a bird. It has an amazing sense of character to it, though sketched in just a few lines.

Rosie watches as she continues, 'Then on Sunday Josh had football, of course. He has to play in the under-thirteens *and* the under-fifteens so there goes half the day, but then we —' She stops. David's vague attention has been completely diverted from her to the view outside the window, where a bird has flown into a tree.

Rosie follows his gaze then looks back to her colleague, waiting. After a full minute, David faces her again. Realising the list of weekend activities is over, he offers up what he knows is an inadequate reply, 'That's a lot. Pretty busy.'

Rosie smiles, nearly forgiving.

He adds, 'I don't know how you do it.'

Rosie looks back out the window. 'What bird was that?'

'A black-faced cuckoo-shrike.'

'How can you tell that from here?'

'The way it shuffles its wings when it lands.'

Rosie looks out at the grey and black bird and shrugs, unimpressed, dismissive. 'It's never just a blackbird with you, is it?'

She disappears behind their divider, then David sighs. He pulls the tray of envelopes towards him and starts to open them.

Then he says very softly, as he looks back out the window at the bird, 'It's a blackbird if it's a blackbird.'

And he smiles.

The phone rings. 'Vic Land and Water Care, David Thomas speaking.'

There is no response for a few moments and then, just as he is about to hang up, he hears a call in the background:

a crow call; a Torresian crow – *Corvus orru*, found only in the northern parts of Australia. The caller must be a birder.

David's heart leaps a little. Someone has seen something! The crow's call is a sharp and harsh *Ar-ar-ar*. It is its aggressive call, probably defending food from a rival. It might be picking at something dead beside the road; it sounds too close to the caller to be in a tree. There is traffic noise as well; a heavy truck goes by and David remembers when he last heard that bird call and that type of engine – it was when he'd passed a troop carrier filled with young soldiers in camouflage uniforms, with short, tight haircuts and wearing wraparound sunglasses. And carrying guns. Army. Army town.

Townsville, David thinks. No, wait . . .

He hears another call, though this time not a bird's. It's a man making a faux bird-call sound, like a mix between a ringing phone and an old ham actor rolling his r's as some form of voice warm-up exercise.

It's Don Barrellon. And if anybody should have been a ham actor, it is Don.

David has known him for nearly fifteen years. Don runs birding boat trips out to the continental shelf off Wollongong on the New South Wales south coast. When they first met, David couldn't quite believe Don wasn't putting on an act. A large man with a large beard and a large personality, he seemed like the creation of an over-enthusiastic actor, one who was playing Falstaff in an old Illawarra Steelers Rugby League jersey and track pants, and an accent as broad as his stomach. But Don is real and so is his love affair with birds and his knowledge of the creatures. He took to David because David is very good at listening, and if there is anything that Don loves more than birds, eating, wine and the sound of his own voice, it is being listened to.

His bird call is a signal he gives when he has seen something he thinks is special and wants a few of his favourites to know about it before anyone else.

The first time David heard it was via a phone call from Don when a wandering albatross had drifted in. Even now, David thinks it odd that a living creature would fly from the other side of the world to come to Wollongong. Not that he will ever tell anybody that – least of all Don. Just as he has never told Don that he had seen the wandering albatross a fair while before Don had given David his bird-call signal.

David doesn't wait for him to speak. 'Don, what's that crow doing?'

There comes a chortle that sounds like the fat old actor who used to sell Heinz tomato soup in television commercials. 'Well, what do you think he's doing, Dave?'

'It's hopping about by the side of the road over . . . a dead possum.'

There's a pause, then a crow call and then an abrupt, 'Well, bugger me! It *is* a possum. I thought it was a cat. You're in form, Dave.'

'Don! Long time; how've you been? What are you doing in Townsville?'

There's a disgruntled sigh from Don before he speaks again. 'Well, now, nobody likes a smart-arse.' Then he laughs. 'In very good form. I've been good; good and busy. Listen, I'm just giving you the nod on a sighting of a pale pygmy magpie goose up here, north of Port Douglas; I'm driving up to see it now.'

'A *what*? *Really*? Sure it's not a green-freckled?'

'I dunno . . . Thought that at first, but it was Bill Matthews – he brings the minibus up every year. From Adelaide. Bunch of oldies, but they know what they're doing usually. They saw it this morning, halfway to Mossman. Jeanne Gallie was up there and she just called me. And David – they heard from Neil.'

'Neil?'

'Yeah. He left any messages for you?'

David pauses a moment. He reads the notes stuck on his computer screen. *David – PPMG here. Neil – call.*

'Shit.'

'I thought you didn't have a tick on it. 'S why I rang.'

'Shit,' David says again. He is senseless with indecision and frustration. 'Shit.'

There is another pause. Don begins to sign off. 'Call me if you come up here.'

'Call me if you see it,' David gets in just before Don gives his bird call again and hangs up.

David stares at nothing. 'Shit!' Louder this time.

Rosie tentatively pokes her head up over the divider. 'Are you all right?'

David doesn't hear her so she repeats the enquiry, louder.

'Fine. Thanks,' he says, picking up a filled-in form, at first trying to decipher it, then just pretending to decipher it.

Shit, he thinks. Then shakes his head firmly. He brings up a graph on his computer screen, looks at his watch then back to the form. At his watch. At the clock. At the screen.

He logs into his bank account. It's a pretty sad sight, but there is some credit available. He brings up a travel site and starts typing, *Origin: Melbourne. Destination: Cairns.*

There's a flight at eleven to Sydney and then an onward flight at two to Cairns. He could be there before dark. He looks up car hire for a four-wheel drive. Bloody expensive. It's ridiculous.

He goes back to his envelopes and pulls out another form but, like a man with a persistent itch, he can't settle. He glances at the calendar and remembers something.

Shit, he thinks again and kicks the desk leg. Quickly lowering his head before Rosie can respond, he picks up the telephone and dials.

'Hi, is Genevieve Forti there, please?' David keeps his back determinedly turned, but he can almost feel Rosie's stare.

'Hello?'

He hunches closer to the phone and speaks quietly, 'Hi, Genevieve. It's David. David Thomas.'

Genevieve laughs. 'Hi, David Thomas. I do know which David. Didn't we sleep together last week?'

David almost winces. 'Well, yeah. Of course. And, um, yeah. It was lovely. You were lovely.'

'*Were*?'

'*Are*, of course. You are. Um . . . This thing on Thursday night, with your friends . . .'

'Yes . . .' Genevieve's tone doesn't give much away.

'Is it, um . . . ? I know it's important to you.'

'Yes.'

David struggles through the silence and the building tension. 'I just might have to go away. Only might.'

'Only might,' Genevieve says. 'So, is there a choice here? Have you got appendicitis or something? Not sure if it's going to perforate? Or is your mother on her deathbed somewhere?'

David hesitates, a bit taken aback by the contrast between the neutrality of her voice and the sharpness of the words. 'My mother's already dead,' he says, without thinking.

'Oh. I'm sorry.' There is an apology in her tone, but one that only admits fault knowing the other is at greater fault. Then there is a pause. Genevieve breaks it first. 'So?'

'So, it sounds like I should come.'

'No, you *shouldn't* come; it would have been nice if you had *wanted* to come. What is it you "might" have to do?'

David screws up his face, knowing he is wrong, already hating himself but unable to stop. 'There's a bird I want to see.'

'A bird.'

'I haven't seen it before.'

'What, and it only shows itself on a Thursday night?'

'It's in Cairns. Well, north of Cairns . . . I'll be back by Saturday.'

'Cairns? A bird?' Genevieve is incredulous.

David lets his words sit.

'God. The scary thing is I actually believe you!'

David waits, hopeful.

'Well, hey – don't come back on my account. There might be a possum you need to check out. Or an island resort. I mean, if you can just fly to Cairns for a weekend, why wouldn't you want to get out on the reef? Have a strawberry daiquiri or two, find Nemo. It's meant to be beautiful out there. I wouldn't know myself.'

'Nemo's a fish,' he says, idiotically. 'Why would I want to go to see a fish?' When he hears the sigh of exasperation at the other end of the phone he tries to back-pedal. Or at least buy some time. 'I haven't decided whether to go or not.'

'So you rang me for what? To take me with you? That doesn't seem to have come up.'

David is silent.

'Then why? To give you what – permission? For me to say, "No, that's fine. I don't mind what you do, don't worry about my dinner and my friends," who I told about you because I thought I might have actually met someone halfway fucking decent and reliable?'

Wincing and not unsympathetic, David lets her words wash over him. He's heard similar before.

CHAPTER TWO

David knocks on the thin partition meant to divide boss from worker, private from public. Being slightly lower than David's height, it does neither.

'Yep?' Maggie is going through a mass of papers on the table with a keen young intern, Daisy.

'Hi, Maggie. When does this job have to be finished again?'

Maggie looks at the papers all around her. 'This job is never going to be finished. What you mean is, "When are they going to stop paying us?"'

David offers her a vague apologetic gesture. 'Well, yes.'

'Maybe when everything is extinct, or everything is GM whether we like it or not, or when some sound bite or election bribery transforms our crap little amount of money into something decent, or maybe even tonight when I have to submit this yearly funding application report I can't finish writing because my stupid computer that they said they'd upgrade "as soon as possible" three months ago crashed and the technical department has been outsourced and —' She glances at Daisy, all lipstick and eagerness, then stops and looks at David. 'Why, David?'

'I just need a couple of days off. If I leave now, I could be back on . . .' David mentally calculates, 'Monday. Leave without pay.'

Maggie gestures towards the papers.

David pleads, 'It's barely two days . . . There's a bird I've got to see.'

Maggie's shoulders slump, almost defeated already. Then she makes a little jutting movement with her chin. David knows she'll turn to her other computer, her laptop.

She turns to her laptop. 'A bird, huh?'

He nods.

'What's it called?'

'Pale pygmy magpie goose. PPMG.'

'Sounds like an accounting firm. Wikipedia okay?'

'It should give you an idea.'

'So sure of yourself, David.' But she's smiling. It's a game and it's obvious she likes him, or something about him – something that if she took the time she'd be interested in trying to uncover. But she realises she doesn't have that much time and she juts her chin out a bit further. 'This thing better be special . . .'

David gives her a look that says, *It is*.

'It *is* an accounting firm!' Maggie says, scanning the screen. 'And some other silly bloody thing: a media management group in Beverly Hills and a . . .' She clicks onto something else and gives a hoot. 'A nice big blackfella with bad ears. Good suit, though. Oh, the joys of a browse on the web.'

David stares at her.

'He's a boxer and he's had his fiftieth birthday party and your PPMG hosted it for him. Nah, they hosted the official after-party. Wanker. Oh well. Evander Holyfield. And he's even got a foundation named after him. His ears – his ears really are bad.'

'One was bitten.'

'What?'

'One was bitten in a fight.'

Maggie looks up at him.

'A boxer called Mike Tyson bit his ear.'

'True?'

He nods.

'You blokes. A fella bit my ear once. Well, he nibbled it. On a date. Thought I should return the favour.'

David looks at her pen. She twirls it a little. Not the whole way around.

'Thank God I had a look down his ear first. Wasn't pretty – put me off custard for a while.'

David makes a face.

'Oh yeah, it's all right for you. You blokes want us girls to go all *Star Trek* on your bits and pieces. Boldly go where no girl should ever go. Here's your bird.'

Maggie twirls the pen between her fingers. Still not the whole way around. 'It's rare.'

'Very rare. Endangered.'

'Can see that. What makes it different from the pale pygmy goose?' She's looking at another webpage now.

'Well, it's more colourful. Predominantly white with blue and green markings and an orange bill. It's got a dark nape flecked with yellow. Iridescent green in the mating season, but other times a pale yellow.'

Maggie nods. 'You still seeing that nice Italian girl? What's her name . . . Jenny?'

'Genevieve.'

'Yeah. She ever bitten your ear?'

'No.' He suddenly feels something nearing shame. 'She's not likely to be biting anything of mine in the near future. Or ever, really.'

Maggie stops twirling the pen and shakes her head. 'She was really nice that time she came in to meet you for lunch. What's a dabbling duck?'

'It's a water bird that feeds from the surface, or just below. It doesn't dive, but the PPMG isn't really a part of that group – it's got lineage from a Gondwanan waterfowl. And it sings.'

Maggie looks at him. 'You making this up?'

'Want to check on Wikipedia? It sings, it's the only waterfowl that sings. A very special bird.'

'That girl Genevieve and her not biting you in the foreseeable future – or ever . . . That got anything to do with the singing goose?'

David just looks at her and repeats almost helplessly, 'It's a very special bird.'

He glances at her hand. If she twirls her pen all the way around in a circle, flipping it gently between her fingers like a marching-band leader flipping a baton, then he'll be okay.

She flips the pen – but not all the way. 'I'm not filling in one extra form for you. Not one word. Forge my signature if you have to.'

'I'll do it all.' David moves to the cupboard and finds the leave forms. He smiles at Maggie. 'Thanks, Maggie. You're a brick,' he says, before starting to walk away.

'A brick. Great,' Maggie mutters after him, deadpan. Then, louder, 'Don't you get tired of just wanting to tick stuff off? You ever want to stop long enough to really get to know one thing?'

He stops and looks back. 'Does anyone, Maggie? You can see things, know what someone or something will do. But does anyone ever really *know* one thing?'

Daisy looks back and forth between them.

'You know, my dad travelled all over – never settled for years,' says Maggie. 'Until he ended up in a village in Thailand watching some old guy fishing. The old guy caught a big fish and he was so happy.'

David stands with the leave forms in his hand.

'Sure, it was a big fish, but this old guy seemed so happy. My father went and asked him how long he'd been waiting to catch the fish.'

There is a silence. Then Daisy says, 'How long?'

'Well,' says Maggie, 'the old guy thought a little and took the hook out of the fish and held it up and then looked at my dad and said, "For a fish like this I waited sixty years." Then he looked at the fish and said almost to himself, "Sixty years." And then let the fish go.'

'Why did he let the fish go?' asks Daisy.

'Because he said he suddenly understood the fish. And he understood that all he wanted to do was catch it, not eat it. The river was full of little fish he could eat almost any time. But that old guy got to know the big fish and himself, what he wanted. So he let it go.'

21

'What did your dad say?' asks David.

Maggie doesn't say anything for a moment and Daisy looks between her and David again.

Maggie takes a deep breath. 'He said he didn't know whether the old guy was wise or a bloody fool but that he knew it was time to come home and stop wandering.'

'You keep moving, you keep learning . . .' David says.

'Isn't that just skimming the surface of knowing something?'

'It's only a few days.' He smiles. 'And it's a bird, not a fish.'

She does the thing with her jaw, jutting it out. 'You're being a dabbling duck – just interested in the surface, not what's down below.'

David stares back.

'One day, David Thomas, Mister Bird Know-it-all, you're going to chase something and actually find it. And you're going to have to decide whether you really understand what finding it means. It's the old-guy-and-the-fish moment. Maybe this singing goose of yours is going to make you decide if you really want to learn.'

She looks at him and he sees something in her eyes that he has never seen before. She's looking right at him, as if she's trying to sense his essence. Like a birder checking a bird they haven't seen before. She stops jutting her chin and the pen makes a full circle in her hands. Then Maggie winks at Daisy. 'Bloody whitefellas. Always wanting to go walkabout. Bloody unreliable.'

Rosie is waiting back at the cubicle.

David shuts down his computer and puts his jacket back on, then tries a joke. 'Maggie's the only person I know who can panic in slow motion.'

'She's not letting you go . . . ? Just like that?'

David starts shoving things into a bag. 'Leave without pay. I'll be back on Monday.'

Rosie frowns, cross. 'We want them to renew this project. We have to meet the deadline. It's the best job I've had for ages. I feel like I'm doing something really good.'

'We're compiling reports that nobody's even going to look at. The only way they'll make a national park is if some stupid opinion poll tells them they have to.'

Rosie looks wounded, but stands firm. 'That's cynical.'

Trying to ignore the stab of guilt, David shrugs and buttons his jacket.

'They still need the information,' Rosie says. 'They still need people to try. Walking down the street with protest signs doesn't tell the real picture. The figures tell the real picture.'

David feels mean. 'I know. You know I care. And God – I need the job too. I'll be back on Monday.'

He walks back to the tram the same way he walked to work, still clocking birds. The silvereyes have gone, but a willie wagtail is on the park lawn, doing its signature dance, desperately trying to draw attention away from its partner's nest for an oblivious audience of passers-by.

David sees a tram coming and, surprisingly for a usually slow mover, runs fast to catch it.

His flat is above and behind a shop. The entrance is actually at the back of the shop, reached by a small lane off the side street. This adds about five minutes to the walk from his flat to the tram stop, which is right outside the shopfront. David has lived there for many years and seen shopkeepers come and go. When the system works, the shopkeepers are able to use David's downstairs kitchen and outside bathroom, and he uses their entrance.

When he first found the place, the shop and flat were both owned by the proprietors of Mahanis' Pet Supplies, a family-run pet shop. David had always hated the idea – and usually the reality – of caged birds, but the family was eccentrically endearing, and loved their pets so much they often adopted them when they couldn't face selling them.

He had seen Mr and Mrs Mahanis and their daughters refuse to sell pets to customers they thought weren't 'right' for an animal.

David had an unrequited crush on their eldest daughter, Eirene, for a time, and still smiles at a memory of her explaining falsely and at length why a particular customer just wasn't a good enough fit for her favourite hermit crab. The crab hadn't moved during its viewing for the potential sale, so Eirene had 'translated' its behaviour to the man and his daughter.

'Put your hand in again and we'll see if he's getting used to you . . . Oh no, oh, that's not good. Sorry, you've upset him . . . What's wrong with you today, Hermie?'

The little girl removed her hand.

Eirene carried on, 'He's very nervous, shy, but also, I have to confess, aggressive. He was treated badly as a little crab and now . . . Well, he finds it hard to like people. It's so sad. I think Hermie's incapable of love.'

The little girl looked increasingly doubtful as she listened to Eirene wax lyrical about the joy the right pet can bring, before being sent away with a goldfish she didn't really like but which Eirene assured her was more capable of loving eight-year-old girls than any other fish, more capable in fact than any other marine creature she had ever known.

Eirene had married years ago and taken a position at the Werribee Zoo, where she now managed its captive breeding programs, established to rescue endangered species from extinction. The Mahanises' second daughter, Zoe, was finishing an Arts/Law degree in between stints of volunteer work at refugee camps around the world, happily slaughtering chickens and goats to feed the hungry. David's friendship with the whole family had gradually enlightened him about the world of animal and human interaction.

The very elderly Mahanis parents had finally retired, worn down not so much by their age as by the battle against the proliferation of chain pet stores in shopping malls, and by the couple's increasing inability to sell anything as they deemed more and more people unfit for pet ownership. They had packed up their menagerie and taken it home to Glenroy, where David still visited them from time to time. They had let him stay in the flat for as long as he wanted with low rent in exchange for his agreeing to share his bathroom and kitchen with the new tenants of the shop. They also left him Mr Peachy.

During the Mahanises' occupancy, David had grown very fond of Mr Peachy, their tame and talkative cockatiel. It had its own cage, but the door was never closed and it treated David's flat as part of its territory. It would follow him up the staircase behind the shop's back door and into the light and spacious multipurpose room, or down the short hall to the kitchen, where an old, unusable wood-fired stove left just enough space for an electric cooker, a narrow bench and a table with two chairs.

Today, a fridge lives with the washing machine and the shower in the lean-to shed outside the back door. And leaning against the lean-to is the toilet, the plank door only big enough to conceal the midsection of a seated person. When David was seated, Mr Peachy would often perch on top of the door and offer him words of encouragement, and pompous discouragement to any potential bird visitors.

The shop downstairs is currently a gift shop selling scented candles and recycled retro homewares. The business is owned by a stockbroker's wife, helping to ease her husband's tax problems, and staffed by a self-identified interior decorator called Janice. As David passes through the shop he thinks of the Mahanises, missing them. He waves a brief hello to Janice, busy with a customer.

'I really think you'll love this collection of pillowcases with the elegant dancing-bear motif – because *I* love them and you seem to be very similar in your tastes to me.'

The customer, a woman with ironed-straight blonde hair and a face graced with a surgeon's refinements, nods back.

'You know,' says Janice, 'eclectic everyday quirky.'

'Yes, yes, yes. The elegant dancing bear,' says the customer.

David shivers a little and heads through the back door and upstairs. He opens his door and feels a pang for Mr Peachy, even though two years have passed since the bird died at a great age. David can clearly remember the morning he found Mr Peachy on the sofa. Still and hunched, as if only playing dead, ready to bounce up and prattle.

He had held the tiny bird in his hand, felt its warmth; Mr Peachy must have only just died. He cupped the creature in his hands for a good while; he didn't know how long exactly, but long enough for the warmth to go and the body to stiffen.

No movement.

No life.

Mr Peachy.

He thought of what the Mahanises would have done. Probably weep. But David hadn't. He'd held the bird's body and looked at it. No, he wouldn't weep; he was too busy trying to understand something. It was just a bird, and a fairly common one. But it was also Mr Peachy. His conflicting feelings had unnerved him slightly and he couldn't quite explain why.

Now, for some reason, he suddenly thinks of Genevieve Forti. He knows something has passed and he tries to explain to himself why he feels a catch in his chest. He stands still for a moment, and then shakes his head and moves over to his desk.

The big main room is still full of birds, though non-living ones; fine drawings, rough sketches and beautifully rendered watercolours, one of which lies half-done on the table beneath the window, surrounded by tubes of paint, coloured inks, crayons and pens. Another, in a wooden frame, sits by a window. It's a painting of a cockatiel: Mr Peachy. David doesn't look but he knows it's there and he nods his head like the pleasant looking blonde actor from *I Dream of Jeannie*, dispensing some bad magic.

Then he thinks, she did it with arms folded. So he does that too, and laughs a little.

He also has a collection of prints of Australian birds; some look like the rescued items from the op shop they actually are, while others – gifts – are museum quality, signed and numbered. There are also various Gould League certificates, including one from his childhood, a brightly coloured detailed print on glossy paper, with his name printed neatly in the space for the new junior member. There are collections of bird magazines, books on birds, plants and trees, as well as lots of rolled-up maps.

David rushes about, experienced and quick at packing a suitable-for-air-travel swag. He stops to place the notebook containing his tram bird list onto a neat pile of similar notebooks. Next to that pile are other piles, labelled back through the last twenty years. He grabs a smaller bag, a backpack, into which he puts three empty field notebooks, a battered old ornithology guide, a small telescope and tripod, his larger pair of binoculars and a watercolour set with paper. Finished, he does a mental then visual check of the room, looks in his pack to confirm he has his smaller binoculars and a pen, as well as his wallet, then locks the door and leaves.

CHAPTER THREE

Clare wakes early. There is no curtain or blind on the window, so she can see that it is nearly dawn. She sits up in the single bed and looks out beyond the concrete verandah to a strip of dewy lawn and a grassy bank barely withstanding the encroachment of tropical flora – short and tall trees seemingly being strangled by vines, with various ferns and large-leafed plants covering the ground underneath them. There are flowers on some of the vines and plants, but the overall picture is one of dense greens and light playing within, backlighting some leaves to a pale yellow or pushing others into cool blacks. The strip of grass is healthy, no patches of straggling cooch.

As Clare is wondering who does the gardening and mows the lawns, a wallaby hops into the window-framed view and starts eating the grass. She makes an involuntary cry of delight and watches it, smiling, until her eyes are drawn away by birds flying into the frame, landing then also hopping on the lawn. A lizard cautiously tests its surroundings, coming inch by inch from its hole under the verandah into the patch where the early morning sun is hitting, near the bird bath.

Clare's smile gradually fades and she stretches. She wears a loose T-shirt over a pair of cotton pyjama pants. Her hair tangled, her eyes tired, she looks as well as she feels in the narrowing timeframe before she turns forty.

The room is mostly empty of signs of habitation. There are two pictures, one for each full wall. The other walls have the window and the door. One picture is a large-scale map of the local area, the other a print of a village in Italy – Bianco, sitting by the sea. It's a mixture of old grey and white buildings, of cobblestones and wooden trellises standing out against the brilliant blue of the water and richness of the sky.

Clare's suitcase lies open, its rummaged-through but as yet unpacked contents spilling out onto the old and oft-waxed floorboards. Sharing the space is a large old rug, complementing yet not matching the upholstery of the single chair, its wooden arms mostly covered by Clare's black coat, jumper and scarf. Her shoes discarded beneath.

She gets up and wanders off to the bathroom. But for her, the house is empty. Sitting on the toilet, she can reach the vanity cupboard under the washbasin. She opens it and idly inspects its contents. It is full. At the front are the products her father must have been using recently. Deodorant, soaps, various shaving implements, a jar of Proraso shaving cream. She remembers the smell – medicinal, sharp and clean – and the hugs her father would give her. 'Nice and smooth?' he would ask when she was a little girl. Then he would gather her in his arms and hold her close.

She remembers the last time he called to her. He was an old man and his last shave had missed some of his stubble. When he held her close she felt it scratch against her own cheeks. The smell of Proraso had seemed a little incongruous, as if the astringency of the cream lay uncomfortably on the old man's skin.

Decay. Clare thinks she could easily cry at that memory but she doesn't. Instead she looks at the creams and unopened toiletry gift packs in the cupboard. There is one gift pack in particular that she is sure she gave her father for Christmas five or six years ago. One of the creams is from a pharmacy. Clare reads the label: *Fatty Ointment, Mr Antonio Cirillo. Use sparingly as required on affected areas.* She looks at her father's name for a long moment,

Antonio Cirillo. She can't think of anyone who would ever call him Antonio. Maybe Nonna when she pretended to be cross with him. In their family it was always Tony. Antonio. The formality of the medication label lifted from the bureaucratic files of the health system and applied without knowledge of who the man really was, strikes her as odd. Antonio. She looks at the cream. She has no idea what it would have been used for.

Long finished on the toilet, she wipes herself, pulls up her PJs and washes her hands. Then empties the cupboard.

Behind her father's things are more lotions and potions from her grandfather's time. There are long-out-of-date medicines and shaving implements, including a cutthroat razor and various early electric shavers. Bandages, bandaids, incomplete first-aid kits and, at the very back, some of her nonna's things. Toilet water and Yardley talcum powder, Italian salves and potions.

Clare picks up a tin, circular, gold-orange, with gold and silver laurels around the side and top. A regal-looking man with a wide drooping white moustache peers out from the lid. Rawleigh's Antiseptic Salve. She can remember seeing this tin before – or one like it. She can hear her father's laughter then his loud voice. 'Here he comes! He's here! Nonna, he's here. Your man with the case!'

Clare and Ollie had run to the window to see the stranger who their father was talking about. To see who was arriving at dusk. Nonna had shushed their father when he let out a great bark of laughter, followed by, 'Quick, it's the man with the potions!'

The Rawleigh's man. A neat, slender man with his singlet showing under his short-sleeved white shirt, both singlet and shirt were tucked into his pressed grey trousers, which ended slightly above his ankles and black shoes. His hair was carefully combed over to one side and a thin moustache of sweat showed above his lip. He looked to the window and smiled at the two children then nodded his head slightly. When Nonna opened the door he had smiled at her too. And his lips had parted and the straightest, whitest teeth beamed like a lighthouse to ships in a dark night.

Ollie had giggled, Clare had just stared. Her father had laughed.

'It's the Rawleigh's man!' he said.

'Hello there,' said Nonna.

'Hello there,' the man with the case had said, and a moth had floated on to his forehead then bounced off. Then he smiled again.

'Hello,' Nonna repeated. 'An orange tin, please.'

'Just one of the salve?'

'Please.'

'Two happy little faces in the window,' he said as he placed his case on the step and took out a bright burnt-orange tin.

'Yes.'

The man gave the tin to Nonna and then took from his shirt pocket a silver pen, which glinted as he wrote on a small black pad.

'Yes. You are well?'

The neat man carefully tore off a receipt and handed it to Nonna as if it were a rose. 'Always well when I'm out and about and seeing happy faces.'

'Good.'

'Thank you very much and we'll see you next month.'

'That will be . . .' Nonna paused. 'Nice. Nice.'

The neat man packed away his case and then turned to the little faces in the window. Ollie got such a fright he ducked down in convulsive giggles. Clare stared back.

'Oh, only one left in the window now!' the Rawleigh's man exclaimed. 'Goodbye, little one. Be good and I will see you again!'

And the Rawleigh's man flipped his glinting silver pen in the air and caught it in his pocket. He picked up his case and walked across the grass before disappearing into the dark. Into the night. Into the forest.

Clare had looked out into the evening darkness. 'Who is the Rawleigh's man?'

Her father had explained, 'The bringer of potions and magic salves.'

Nonna gently poked him in the stomach. 'You shush. He is a nice man and the ointments are good.' She turned to Clare. 'Your father! He is a cheeky boy!' And she poked him again. 'The Rawleigh's man sells the tins. He travels around selling the tins.' She held the tin down in front of Clare. 'This tin.' It was shiny and orange and gold.

'Where did he go?' Clare asked.

'Off to sell some more,' said Nonna.

'Off into the dark, out into the jungle, braving the dangers with his tins of orange and gold!' said her father, grinning.

Nonna half giggled and clucked, 'Your father!' And she stroked the back of her granddaughter's head.

Clare looks at the tin in her hands now. She can remember thinking that the neat man, the Rawleigh's man, was quite heroic, marching through the darkness with his pressed trousers and shiny pens, walking through the jungle, selling his tins.

She holds the tin and the Proraso and puts them to one side, before continuing to clear the cupboard.

When it is empty, its contents almost cover the bathroom floor. Clare stretches then decides she will sort it out later. She will probably end up just putting it back into the cupboard again, for the time being at least, she thinks, and she walks out.

Halfway down the hall she stops and looks into her father's room. It is the opposite of hers. A double bed with maybe only a third left for sleeping, the rest completely covered in books and magazines, photographs, notebooks and old coffee cups. The standard lamp on the floor next to the bed is plugged into an extension cord that snakes its way across the middle of the room. Stacks of magazines stand about the floor in an apparent attempt at tidiness. Failed tidiness, Clare thinks. There are also piles of clothes, gumboots, bird books, maps, coats and an old computer. She looks on from the doorway. She has no desire to enter her father's space so she moves on.

In the kitchen Clare makes toast from a loaf she brought with her and eats it with homemade jam from the pantry. She looks around. Like the bathroom cabinet, the kitchen contains the detritus of three generations.

She wanders through the rest of the house. Every room is full of stuff as though still lived in, as if people might come home at any minute. Well, one eccentric man, at least, and his eccentric mates, judging by the turn-out at the funeral.

She stands in the lounge room. The decorating of the house seems to have halted in the seventies, when Nonna died, though a form of nesting has continued since then. The first layer is the one she remembers from the holidays when she came back here to visit: Poppa's fruit-box collection, which covers all of one wall and half of the next. Old-fashioned tins of fruit. Souvenirs from other fruit-growing regions as well as bottles of wine, musical instruments, and books, masses of books. Endless pieces of paper, some covered in her father's notes, almost illegible. Some are pages torn from variously shaped notebooks; notes are also written on the backs of envelopes, on paper serviettes and the reverse sides of bills.

Above the door hangs the tin sign from the first cannery: *Cirillo Fruits*. There is something about the colours, or perhaps the quality of the printing, that sets it in a particular time and place. Like the old Technicolor films. Panavision, thinks Clare vaguely. Kodacolor, Kodachrome. For Clare that time and place are the childhood holidays she spent here.

She remembers swimming, jungle adventures – jungle, not rainforest. Clare smiles. She and Ollie were probably hunting lions and tigers and bears, not echidnas or wallabies. She recalls swinging out over the river on a rope swing. Or was that an old ad on the television? Her memory seems to display that recollection in Technicolor. But they had no television then – she can't recall ever watching television in this house. Instead, there was playing under the sprinkler, summer storms, ice creams. Choc wedges. Eskimo Pie. Surely they don't call them that still? Wouldn't that be like having a Negro milkshake? But there never was a Negro milkshake. Maybe in Italy. Or is that word French? She must learn French. Italian.

As Clare's mind floats, her eyes gradually focus on the closed box in the middle of the lounge-room floor: a *Bonacci's Best Bananas* box with a note sitting on top. She retrieves it.

Hey Clare,
This is all I want, but if there's anything you want in here I'm happy to have an arm wrestle over it.

Clare makes a face. Ollie always wins.

I took something for the children so they will remember their Aussie Pop. I couldn't tell what was Dad's or Poppa's most of the time, and what should go to the wayward brother and cousin/s? Hopefully you paid more attention?!

Clare rolls her eyes. Gee, thanks, Ollie.

I rang all the people Dad seemed to have coming to stay and cancelled all. There wasn't a heap – mostly his friends, judging from the responses.
I will keep executing from over here. You'll have to do the electricity and stuff – I didn't know how long you would stay. I really don't mind if you get a box of stuff for yourself, close the door, take the next plane home and sell it all, the house and everything in it.

*Can you look after my box until Christmas? We will
try and come* en famille *then. Thanks, Bear.*

Love ya,

Oll

Clare sits down on an over-plump floral, wide-armed
lounge chair, sinking deep into where the springs used to
be. She shuffles back out and perches on the edge.

She looks at the box then at the rest of the room, packed
with stuff, then back at the box. How did he manage to
keep it to one box?

Next to the chair is a guitar. Clare picks it up and
plucks at the strings while still focusing on the box. Before
any melody can start, she puts it down, too curious. She
kneels down and opens the box. A burnt-red Atomic coffee
machine, wrapped in a bit of bubble wrap. Two tin toys – an
orbiting spaceman and the other a merry-go-round with
chain chariots flying out as it rotates. Her father's toys,
brought out by his Italian aunts when they came to stay.
As he got older he talked more about his aunts, as older
people do, their childhoods somehow moving back to the
forefront of the mind as the brain completes its life cycle.
They were always the *Italian* aunts; Clare can't remember
their names. Are they still alive? They would be in their
eighties at least. They do have that Mediterranean diet on
their sides, though, thinks Clare. Has someone told them

about her dad, about their little nephew Tony? Who should she call, write to? She must ring Ollie and check, though the chances of him knowing anything are probably slim. But surely that's an executor's job? Of course it's the boys with the power and the girls with the packing.

She berates herself. How slack, she thinks. You were happy to avoid being the executor; you offered to pack up the house, or at least go through it. Maybe she should just do what Ollie says, gather a 'best of' box to take back to Melbourne and go via the estate-agent's office. When the house sells she will be able to afford the odd holiday up here, on the coast, at one of the resorts with pools as moats and buffet breakfasts. Clean sheets, no dust and no stuff.

She looks around the room again. It's bigger than the bathroom cabinet. How to begin? Her eyes catch upon various objects, some vaguely familiar, others with strong memories attached. Reminders of the highs and lows of moments in her own and others' lives, each one a fresh revelation leading to a hundred other memories. She sits back, overwhelmed. She could spend the rest of her days like an archaeologist on a dig of her earlier life and what came before her being.

Getting up, she goes to the kitchen to make herself a drink. Looking through her package of various herbal and organic tea bags she remains uninspired, until a thought – coffee.

She looks in the freezer. It is full of not only good coffee, but also a wide range of spices – fresh-frozen or home-dried in an assortment of used jars along with store-bought spices of considerable vintage. In the fridge there are also lemon wedges, milk, tomato sauce and chocolate. A packet of licorice-and-chocolate bullets is open for ready access by a fast hand grab. Clare takes some, puts two in her mouth at once. Smiling, she scribbles a note on the back of an envelope, takes the Atomic out of Ollie's box and leaves the note in its place.

She has watched both her grandparents and her parents use the Atomic stove-top espresso maker for as long as she can remember. She shakes some coffee beans into the grinder, still attached to the wall through many paint jobs, cyclones and children.

'Winding the grinder is a time gift from the gods,' Poppa had told her. 'Enjoy it as such. Grind, think, don't think, look at things, don't look. Whatever you want. It's your time gift.'

Later, her father had said a similar thing when she was impatient for the little red man on the traffic signals to turn to green. 'Waiting for the lights to change is a time gift from the world, just enjoy.' At the time, she thought of how Poppa must have said those words to her father, and now he was saying them to her.

Most of the time, as a little girl, she hadn't listened to her father, *wanting* the lights to change. Then, as an adult she was too caught up in thinking about the doctor's appointment or what had been said in the meeting or whether she could afford a car yet. But she had said the same thing when Jas had held her hand, jiggling up and down with childish impatience, wanting to get to wherever it was they were going, wanting to be there already. Then wanting to be at the next place.

'Just enjoy where you are when you're there,' Clare would tell her. 'You can't make the lights change, and you can't cheat or the lights have no purpose. They're here for a good reason. You can't let the people in the car think that it's a prank and that no one needs to stop. They need to see you stop so they'll always stop. Because when a car hits a child: *Bang*.'

Clare keeps grinding the coffee beans. Did Jas appreciate the time gift as she grew older? Or was the lovely simple message so overtold and mixed up with Clare's own stupid fears that she'd made it meaningless? Had she turned the gift into an instruction?

She stops grinding and brings the coffee across to the bench, inhaling the fresh smell, taking a deep breath of it then letting it out as slowly and fully as she can, pushing the last of the air from her lungs, keeping her mouth shut and trying to hold on with no air. One, two, three . . . She makes it to fourteen before her body disobeys her and takes a big breath in then lets out a sigh; a whole-body sigh, all muscles relaxing. Her shoulders drop by six inches. Her face relaxes.

The Atomic coffee-making process is satisfyingly manual: unscrewing the side water cover, shaking it over the sink to tip out any old water, giving it a quick rinse, then filling it with fresh water – just up to the screw – before screwing the lid back on and putting it on the same gas ring it always goes on. Clare firmly grasps the handle and twists until it unlocks, banging it hard against the side of the bin to knock out the old coffee, packed to shape, then refilling it with fresh coffee and locking it back in. She smiles, thinking about her brother packing the box with coffee growing slightly green in the Atomic.

She feels a remnant of the pleasure she felt in one of her many early and short-lived jobs: making the coffees in a lunch bar. One step up from the kitchen hand or dishwasher role she usually took and a few rungs below the waitressing jobs she always applied for but was never given. She would stand behind the machine, juggling froth and flat, banging, locking, pouring, casually moving the jug up and down the steam valve until the milk was just so. She remembers people calling out orders and that handle lock-in moment.

Handles. Why on earth did they get rid of them on pokie machines? Surely that was the pleasure of them? The grasping, the slow pull or the slow then quick, the quick and don't look, the entire arm involved. Why get rid of that? How does pressing a button make you feel you may have some chance of pulling four queens or Aztec gold?

Clare puts her teeth together, her lips drawn back, as she waits for the cup to brew. Where the hell is her brain?

She carries her coffee out to the verandah and sits on the edge, where the concrete meets the grass. She needs to sweep it. She needs to make a list of all the things she must do. Leave the sweeping till last, till the agent comes, then maybe do it again each time people come through. No, she doesn't have to be here for that. Or maybe she should? Maybe she should just settle in, get off the antidepressants, see if she's all right? Brave it here on her own away from her home in the city. And if she's not all right in, say, six weeks, or eight? Then get back on the pills and go home. Or go home anyway and be herself, see if this is her now or whether she's being held in a state of chemical non-panic. Maybe the cyclone's over and she's still holding tight in the dark cellar with cans of baked beans?

Clare sips her coffee. It's delicious. She leans against the verandah post and looks around. Doors open out from all the rooms down one side of the house. Some of the supporting posts are being coaxed to join the forest with tendrils of vines curling upwards around them. A bird is flying about at mid-tree height, performing aerial gymnastics that seem to be purely for joy and for the creation of beauty, until, too curious, Clare gets up and steps slowly closer and she can see the small flying insects that the bird is catching. Lunch.

She sits back on her step, relaxed and sun-stupored, looking at the ants busying themselves about her feet. Are they, too, just in search of food?

CHAPTER FOUR

In the cooler late afternoon she goes for a walk. The track that leads from the house to the lower orchard and the stream is still the same as when she was a child, but the orchard is even smaller than she remembers from her last visit. The rainforest, in contrast, seems bigger. Had she thought it smaller when she first came back as an adult, when her dad had moved back here? Sick of the loneliness and reminders of her mum in their own house, he'd come back to this place, his childhood home. A big, fat, house-sized foetal position where he'd brought all the stuff he and her mum had, planning to sort it out when he got there. But his lifelong love of the natural world had taken up all his time instead. He hadn't so much moved in as brought in more sticks and made himself a nest.

Coming back up the path, Clare walks around the house to the four old pickers' cabins. She pokes her head into a couple. They are each furnished with the bunks she remembers from her childhood, though bunks might not be the right word. Each one consists of canvas stretched across a steel frame. She is reminded of museum visits to reconstructed early Australian orphanages or migrant hostels. Or prisons. That's where they might well have come from. Poppa had probably done a deal with some institution that was closing down, buying them cheaply for his pickers. The bird people her dad had invited up for sleepovers must be made of strong stuff, she thinks.

Old wooden fruit boxes have been roughly arranged as tables and stools between the beds, while other remnants of the cannery business have been used for both practical and decorative purposes: candles in fruit tins and tin signs hanging on the walls.

One shed, the old fruit-washing shed, has been turned into a rough laundry-cum-bathroom, with a sink, an ancient washing machine and a shower in a small, tiled recess. The only shed to have electricity attached, it also has an old fridge, a two-burner stovetop and an electric kettle dating from the eighties in tis second room. Outside, near a shed in a small clearing, is some kind of bush shower: a hose on a post with a large hook secured to the post and a slatted wooden square on the ground beneath it.

A car slows out on the main road. Clare is only dimly aware of it until she hears the sound of tyres crunching on the gravel at the front of the house. She starts a little, never feeling comfortable socialising with strangers. Her instinct is to hide, hoping they will leave a note at the door and go away. Then she remembers that the front door is open. She quickly walks back past the clothesline and through the house.

A man of around her age, perhaps a bit older, whom she vaguely recognises from the funeral and from somewhere else, stands at the door, holding a strange-looking bird. Clare's face remains impassive, giving away nothing of her nerves, or her surprise at the sight of the bird. Or the man. She looks at the two, expressionless.

'Hi,' she says.

The man moves the bird to one arm and holds out a hand. 'Neil. I met you at Tony's – sorry, your dad's funeral. I'm very sorry for your loss. He was a good man. Inspirational.' He speaks in an oddly formal way, as if unused to these kinds of words or feelings.

'Oh, yeah. Hi. Thanks.'

It was the funeral. He had stared at her that day – not in a disturbing way, but with a little more intent than the other mourners. As if he may have expected something. His eyes, she had thought, were quite wary.

Clare looks at the bird, its long legs hanging down from a brown body the size of a small chicken. With large, staring eyes, a straight beak and a long neck something about the bird is not quite right.

'This is Picnic. Mind if I put her down?'

Clare shrugs; of course not.

The bird stands still for a few moments, takes a couple of steps this way and that, then walks to the birdbath in the garden and assumes the personality and mobility of a garden statue.

After a moment, Clare looks back at Neil enquiringly.

'They sometimes call them stone curlews. You can see why.'

Clare waits for more.

'He was your dad's pet.'

'Pet?' Clare is surprised.

'I told your brother about her.'

Thanks again, Ollie, thinks Clare. She looks back to the bird.

'I would have left her here, after . . . after your father passed, but your brother said he didn't know how long it would be till you were back up to sort everything out. She can mostly look after herself but she's got a funny thing with her beak and she's a slow hunter. She can't really fend for herself. Your dad had her from when she was a chick. An abandoned chick.' Neil pauses. 'Hopeless.'

'The bird or Dad?' Clare is confused.

'Your dad.'

'Oh?'

'All talk about keeping everything neutral, only keeping the weeds out. But he could never cut down old George's fruit trees.' He looks at Picnic. 'Could never leave a little bird to die.'

'She's interesting looking,' offers Clare.

'She's a bush curlew. She's always hung around your dad's study or near the bird feeder there,' Neil says, gesturing towards it. He shakes his head, disgusted. 'Bird feeder. I've popped over a few times to fill it, but you really should wean the wild birds off it. Tony thought he was immortal, that he'd always be here to put food out for them.'

'Why is he – sorry, *she*, called Picnic?'

'I don't know. Your father named her. Maybe he was having a picnic at the time?'

Clare nods, feeling awkward; she can't figure out Neil's relationship to her father.

There is a longer pause, Clare wishing she could find a way to end the conversation. She takes a step backwards then stops, hoping Neil will take the hint. The silence lengthens.

'I'm not sure how long I'm staying. I've just come to pack up, really,' she says finally, feeling Neil looking at her. She keeps her eyes on Picnic. 'So maybe it would be better if you took her? I mean, if you'd like her. Did she get used to your place?'

Neil shrugs; neither a yes nor a no. They both watch Picnic poke about at the edge of the verandah.

'You wouldn't keep it?' Neil asks.

'Keep Picnic? No, I just live in a flat. In Melbourne.'

'Not Picnic – all this.' Neil's gesture includes the gardens, the orchard and the house. The property.

Keep it? Clare hasn't let that thought enter her head. It irritates her for some reason and she answers quite sharply, 'What for?'

'It's a beautiful place. It's been in your family for generations.'

'What? It's hardly Downton Abbey!'

Neil looks blank, and Clare feels embarrassed at having revealed her television tastes. Feeling his disapproval, she tries to explain. 'I never lived here and neither did Ollie, my brother. We never grew up here or anything. We never lived here when Dad took it over. My memories are of when my grandparents had it, when it was an orchard with all that lovely fruit, and the pickers coming in season and helping make all the afternoon teas and sitting around singing at night. Not just – whatever it is now: a falling-down house full of too much stuff. It's like everyone left everything here to pick up later —'

'Your dad was making a kind of sanctuary – bird sanctuary – here. It's the edge of the escarpment and the edge of the rainforest. The clearing the orchard created – it's perfect. There're over twenty species of birds that have been sighted on this property.'

'My poppa would've hated to see Dad let his orchard go like this. Poppa loved fruit, Dad loved birds. Now Dad's dead.' Clare feels the tears start pricking her eyes. It's as if only in this moment, hearing herself speak to this man about her father's death, does the choice before her seem real. She can smell the Proraso, feel her father's half-shaved chin, remember that time in the hospital when he had bent down to her and whispered, 'See – nice and smooth,' and held her. And then, in gentle Italian, '*La mia bambina, la mia ragazza, mia dolce ragazza.*' She hears him laugh and sees the books on his bed, the coloured fruit tins; she can *feel* him. Shit. She hates it, hating her tears in anger but even more in self-pity.

Neil grants her a moment and then asks, neutrally, 'I thought your dad wanted to leave it to the National Parks or the bird people?'

'He tried. Nobody wanted it for what he wanted them to do with it. Apparently they don't just take anything they're given – there's the running costs and staffing and stuff. It was not, to quote, "a significant enough donation to warrant the diversion of limited funds", blah, blah . . .'

Neil looks at her, not quite believing her words.

Clare tries to be brisk. Brusque. 'Hopefully the new owners will like birds. It's hardly as if someone's going to buy the place and build an office tower, or a resort —'

Neil nods his head slowly. 'They might.'

Clare raises an eyebrow.

Neil shrugs. 'A golf course?'

Clare thinks of the area. Run-down Queenslander houses, small acreage farms, still straggling and struggling along, a few hobby farms, horse paddocks, palliative-care yards for old cars.

'What about the lodges your father started?'

'Lodges? What lodges?'

Neil gestures to the group of sheds. 'The pickers' cabins. Your dad was hiring them out, doing little tours of the place – mostly for birders.'

Lodges! Clare shakes her head, incredulous. 'My brother cancelled all that; he said there wasn't much happening anyway.'

Neil looks disappointed. 'He cancelled? Cancelled! Well.' He stops and Clare looks at him. 'Oh, that's going to be a hassle.' He rubs his temple with a forefinger.

Clare feels herself becoming angry, sick of having to explain herself to this stranger. 'Well, we had to. The house is being sold. It was left to Ollie and me. We are required to do something about it. I don't know anything about birds. Ollie lives in France, so it's even less use to him.' Her voice rises a notch.

Neil nods his head while still scratching his temple. And they look at each other, Clare wishing he would go away. What bloody business of his is any of this?

Neil looks around again, glancing at Picnic, then back at Clare. 'He left you Picnic as well.'

Clare shrugs. 'Fine.' She hates him.

'And I think he meant you to have it – not Ollie Dolly.' Neil pulls out his keys.

Clare stares at the man. 'Ollie Dolly?'

'I knew you when you were little; when you came up on holidays. When your grandpa had the orchard. My dad was a picker. We lived outside Mount Molloy.'

Clare looks at him, interested despite herself.

Neil is self-conscious. 'I know it's been a few years but . . .' His face breaks into a wide crazy-toothed smile. Like the Rawleigh's man's smile.

Clare clocks it. Her own face relaxes a little. 'You're not Murph?'

Neil is straight-faced for a moment. Then he smiles again. 'Murph! *Rack off, Murph!* I haven't heard that for a while. Yes, that's me.'

'I hadn't heard Ollie Dolly for a while, either,' Clare says slowly. 'Or seen the Rawleigh's man smile.'

Neil throws back his head and laughs. 'Out there in the jungle – just him, his case and his teeth. Oh, your father . . .'

Clare's mind again fills with rope-swing memories, but this time including Neil, four school years ahead of her, swinging wildly out over the river, holding her hand to help her over the rocks so they could jump into the water, to be swept down with the current to the green rocks dotted through the river. Her crush on him. She and Neil teasing Ollie Dolly and Ollie teasing back until all three of them were in stitches. She can't help but grin. She studies Neil again now, sees the twinkle in his eye, the humour, the self-consciousness.

'God!' Clare laughs, her face losing its usual reserve, and her eyes shining mischievously. Her laugh is infectious.

Neil nods, waves his keys at her and backs towards his car, making no move to take Picnic. 'How long you about?' he asks.

Still breathing a little heavily from laughing, Clare says, 'Oh, just till I clear things, get stuff sorted. Not that long.'

Neil fiddles with his keys. 'You might find your phone ringing . . . You might, you know. About . . . Well, you'll see,' he says awkwardly, then turns away to avoid any reply.

Picnic walks towards Clare, stares, blinks and then, slowly, unconcernedly, moves back towards the birdbath.

Clare watches Neil's car drive away. Then she hears from inside the house, from her father's office, the sound of a phone ringing. She looks at the departing car and the light cloud of dust left in its wake. Her gaze follows it and then settles for a moment on the deep green of the rainforest. She inhales its richness, the mingling smells of decay and immeasurable fertility. Realising the phone is still ringing, she turns and walks inside.

CHAPTER FIVE

David sits in the middle seat of a row of three, down the back, not far from the toilet. He can't reach his bag and has nothing to read. It is nearly two hours into his second flight. Impatience to arrive has condensed into a kind of internal mantra: *Please let us be there now. Please don't crash or slow down or circle. Please let us be there now.*

His ears are still blocked from the flight before, his hearing a little more muffled than usual. He tries to close his eyes and sleep but feels too squashed.

David is a tall man and not particularly thin, but he has nothing on the man sitting in the aisle seat beside him. Dressed in a suit with his coat on his lap – or what *would* be his lap if he were in a seat that contained him in a respectful way as opposed to one down the back of economy – his body takes up the armrest, never mind his arms. His massive gut seems uncomfortably constricted and he has food stains on the front of his white shirt.

David feels a prick of pity. Maybe the man with the massive gut is a proud man? David hates the idea of a proud man being humiliated. He doesn't know what he means by 'proud' or if there is even a physical type for a proud man.

The man shifts uneasily in his seat. David remembers one of his first birding trips – to the Werribee sewage farm outside of Melbourne. He had been twelve or thirteen years old and had gone there with a kindly, patient and firmly uninterested uncle, who throughout the day had smiled at David and occasionally patted him on the head. This was in between exclamations of delight and groans of anguish as he listened to the races and then the football through tiny white earphones that led to an AWA transistor radio.

It was while his uncle was busying himself in a long-drop toilet and letting out a celebratory half-sung, half-hummed rendition of the Richmond Football Club's song, 'Oh, We're from Tigerland', that David saw the old man. He had tottered to a bench not far from where David was sitting. He was twisted and bent and breathed heavily. The man had sat down, panting, his crooked mouth gaping like a fish freshly landed on a jetty. David had seen him earlier in the day, when the birding group had gathered by a comfort station near the entrance to the farm. He was named Mr Baxter and he had apparently suffered a series of strokes. Some fuss was made of him because it was his first trip with the birding group for some time.

David watched Mr Baxter on the bench as a string of saliva slowly descended from a corner of the old man's mouth while his left hand shook uncontrollably. David felt uncomfortable; he had never seen an adult in such a state before. The man made a sound, a soft little howl. He looked to David, and David, thinking it rude to look back, turned away. Mr Baxter howled a little again. David turned back. He realised that the shaking hand was beckoning him over.

David walked across to the old man and was suddenly gripped with the fear that Mr Baxter would ask him for help going to the toilet. But instead the old man exclaimed in a voice surprisingly clear from a mouth so twisted, 'Lewin's rail! A Lewin's rail!' His finger was pointing to a notepad on his lap. 'First one I've seen here. And I walked nearly two hundred yards by myself to see it. *By myself!*'

A Lewin's rail. It was a good bird to see, a shy bird that hid deep in the vegetation of the sewerage farm and built runways through the undergrowth to scurry around in. A good bird.

Mr Baxter howled softly again and gave a trembling thumbs-up.

He's proud, realised David. Proud of what he's done. David had stared then smiled back. 'That's a good bird.'

Mr Baxter dribbled a bit more and tried to catch his saliva with his other hand. David held out his hanky. The old man nodded. 'Good bird,' he agreed and then said softly, 'beautiful day.'

This was definitely a proud man, David thought. Then he heard his uncle end the happy chorus of 'Oh, We're from Tigerland' with a curlew's cry from the long-drop and, 'Oh, Christ – a protest! A bloody protest!'

David remembers Mr Baxter now as he glances at the man next to him.

When the tired flight attendant finally reaches the back of the plane and offers the passengers a biscuit and a cup of tea, the man refuses. David lowers his own tray table and realises that the man wouldn't have been able to accept – his body is too big to use the tray table.

The attendant stares blankly at them, his eyes blind to his passengers. If he wanted to, he could taunt them with this tiny offering of food, hold it out and then withdraw it; there would be nothing they could do. David looks at him. Surely it must be tempting sometimes? We're helpless, really, he thinks, nested here like ungainly chicks waiting for the parent bird to bring food.

The man with the large gut shifts in his seat again and David feels the whole row heave. He's a bit like a huge show pigeon, David thinks, a Carneau, with its swollen abdomen like the billowing sails of a Spanish galleon. But the show pigeons would be sitting at the front of the plane, at the pointy end. We're more like caged birds, he thinks, trapped.

David remembers the time he worked for a weekend on a chook farm owned by a friend of one of his aunts. There was a boy there, not much older than himself, who would taunt the chickens in their tight cages for no other reason than that he could. He would stare at the caged birds as he collected the eggs and then he would hit the cages, sometimes just as the birds stuck their heads through the bars.

The boy had turned and caught David's eye. 'I saw you – saw you do that,' David had said. And the boy did nothing. He had simply stared back for a very long moment, and then went about his business.

The Carneau man heaves again as he tries to accept a morsel of something in a packet from the flight attendant after all. His tray table is hinged at an alarming angle. David's table also sits oddly, but more because he can't straighten his legs in front of him so it has to balance on his knees.

The flight attendant and David stare at each other and David wonders if the boy in the chook shed had gone on to work in airline services. He is almost waiting for the flight attendant to randomly strike a passenger and then go on his way.

He doesn't strike but he does offer a beverage.

When David is handed his tea, he enjoys a couple of sips, then thinks of his neighbour, realises he couldn't possibly ask the man to move to allow him to go to the bathroom, so doesn't drink the rest.

In the window seat, a man is taking photos of the view below. Nice camera. David can only guess at the scene, not being able to see past the man's head. Oceanside, patterns of the reef, perhaps an island. He assumes that the man is doing his best to imagine himself not on a plane. He has the look of a claustrophobe, enduring discomfort. David has heard that distracting yourself, by looking at a view through a lens for example, you can distance yourself from the reality of where you are. He wonders if the man is trying to distract himself by looking at the view through the lens. Would binoculars work in that way too? Perhaps not; whenever David goes out on a boat he still gets seasick whether or not he uses his binoculars. His thoughts drift further: is it his love of birds or his detachment from all else but himself and the bird he is watching that makes the surroundings seem benign?

He looks away quickly as the man turns from the window and rests his head back. David sneaks another glance at him. He has closed his eyes. He is pale and older than David had first thought. Well, maybe not older, just tired, with dark circles under his eyes and folds in his skin that don't match the usual path of ageing.

David's eyes drop to the camera, which he's holding as if it's an extension of his hands. It has no strap. His hands also look battered and old, dry and age-spotted with raised veins. A doer, David thinks, before he notices the way the man's veins travel up his arms. They are corded, twisted and scarred. He is ill. Emaciated and worn down by his illness and treatment. He might be dying, David thinks. God, I'm here in the middle of two people, one of them is surely killing himself, the other is perhaps being killed by his own body, and I've just spent all my money and put my job on the line by travelling two thousand kilometres to *maybe* see a bird. Christ, he wonders, how many stories is this plane carrying?

The plane banks left then straightens out before descending. Bags are placed back under seats, the flight attendants check that all is in order, that everyone is seated. He anticipates the landing, delayed for a moment by a small bounce, then *wham*, touchdown and hard braking.

When the aircraft doors are opened, David walks down the steps and out onto the tarmac. He loves the tarmac walk. It makes him feel that the plane is real and therefore safer than when he's being funnelled through air-conditioned tunnels to reach the security gates and baggage halls.

Here he is on the ground in the late afternoon. It is hot – winter-tropical hot, the opposite of Melbourne. Bougainvillea climbs over the boundary fences. The individual blooms are beautiful, shockingly bright, but thousands together are accepted as commonplace. For David, though, it is not so much the visual scene as the smell of this place and the sounds that create the very particular moods. He wastes no time in picking out the jet fuel from the natural perfumes and in listening to the birds. Before he reaches the small arrivals hall he has added seven birds to his list.

There's something about the air here, the novelty of being away, that makes him feel somehow more entrenched in Australia than when he's in the cosmopolitan, European-like Melbourne. Not a more real version exactly, as each place is as imposed as the other, but maybe a grass-is-greener version.

He collects his swag from the baggage carousel and makes his way through reunions and parties of holiday-makers. Singlets on buff skins of many shades; old, hairy tattoos; the arms of women who, in cooler climes, would have been covering them since they were thirty. It's whatever works here, David thinks.

He finds the hire-car stand and reports in.

'Now the news for you could be good or it could be bad, or maybe it'll be of no consequence . . .'

David can't hear all the words, lost in the static of the terminal noise and the hum in his ears that is becoming more pronounced. He leans forward, trying to be polite. 'What does that mean?'

'Afraid the car you've ordered isn't available.'

'The four-wheel drive?'

'Not available.'

'So I don't have a car?'

'Well, you do. A Tarago.'

'Pardon?'

'There's no extra cost,' explains the young man, dressed in a corporate take on a Hawaiian shirt.

'I ordered a four-wheel drive.'

The man looks at him as if David is being deliberately difficult. 'I'm sorry, sir. That's all we have available.'

David still can't really hear but watches as the man goes to the wall of keys and looks at the two pairs remaining. He comes back to the bench and begins going through each drawer, carefully checking for other keys.

Trying to be patient, David looks away.

Over the top of the hire-car booth he recognises the familiar flight path of a large honeyeater as it makes its way behind the palm trees, presumably planted to make the car park seem like a welcome to the tropics. Not being native and providing no shade, these trees don't do much for David. But the honeyeater does; its flap-rise-pause-fall, flap-rise-pause-fall a flight pattern common across the ninety species of honeyeater native to Australia. David has seen seventy-one of them; this is his seventy-second.

The man holds out the Tarago keys. He has given up his search to find another car. 'Insurance?' He hands David a sheet explaining the different rates.

David has a quick look. It's complex and expensive so he dismisses the offer. He still hears the hum in his head; it's exacerbated by his blocked ears from the flight. He closes his eyes and works his jaw, then forces out an elongated yawn.

The man behind the counter looks faintly disgusted.

David gives a long sigh; his head hums on.

By the time he dumps his swag in the cavernous people-mover, he has added another ten birds to his list. He shifts the seat back to accommodate his long legs and pulls out his notebook, neatly marking the date for the new trip list and then writing down the location and the birds he's seen here so far today. He then pulls out another, older notebook, containing his Far North Queensland regional life list. He closes his eyes and lets out a leisurely yawn. His ears pop, but the hum is still there.

David puts his binoculars on the seat next to him, fastens his seatbelt and sets off into the evening, suddenly happy.

The car's engine sounds not quite right, like it is about to explode, and it handles the way a slothful boat might, drifting here and there and dipping into the tide. The motion is quite pronounced. David notices that the vehicle smells sadly of disinfectant and bleach. Perhaps, he thinks, if my hearing is going my sense of smell is improving? Does the human body work like that? He takes a deep breath and blows it out. Sickness. The car reeks of illness, like a hospital. You know it's there beneath the chemicals. Maybe the pitching and rolling of the van created the need for the use of bleach and disinfectant.

It strikes him as being less a car and more a cross between a submarine and a cream bun. Why a cream bun? He can't explain but he winds down the window and feels the warm air rush in.

Yes, he thinks, I'm happy. Happy bobbing along the road, bobbing along in search of birds.

He drives on and suddenly, for no particular reason, starts singing 'Oh, We're from Tigerland', oblivious to the car's engine whining like a Stuka dive-bomber on full attack.

CHAPTER SIX

Cairns airport is north of the city, on the flat coastal land beneath the escarpment. The usual mix of Queenslander-style houses and commercial properties are strung out along the road as if someone has just tossed the buildings down without fences, planning or recognition of their surroundings. There is so much land they can do what they like.

The moon shines on the sea, and David stops a couple of times to take in the view. Back on the road he sails past the turn-off to Port Douglas, an old port town turned resort.

In the early days, the port was the main access point for the goldfields and farms in the hinterland, but a series of cyclones destroyed whatever promise it had held for further development. Eventually the town was bypassed by a highway. It was a pleasant enough place in a forgotten-beach-town way until the 1980s, when a resort was opened on its muddy beaches, a palace of indulgence created by one of the decade's great cigar-chomping corporate shysters, Christopher Skase.

David still remembers a birding trip to south-west Victoria he went on when he was about twenty and the words of a very large woman with a minimalist haircut and multiple body piercings who ran a hair salon in Bendigo. They had been discussing Port Douglas and she described the resort as being the hotel equivalent of the bad 1980s big-hair perm. He thought this rather apt.

The port had ridden out the late eighties recession and boomed, while Christopher Skase, having changed the essence of the north, parcelled up as much of his wealth as possible and ended up as a very comfortably-off tax exile in Spain. Chased by debtors and successive governments, he managed to evade them by claiming he had a serious lung condition, until at last, on the eve of yet another extradition attempt, he died of stomach cancer.

Having outlived its creator, the redeveloped port was gradually taken over by a combination of junk-filled tourist shops, 'rustic' shed-construction hotels hosting cane-toad racing for the tourists, and five-star restaurants. Massage parlours, beauty salons and psychic card readers were interspersed with coffee shops good, bad and indifferent. The place rang with accents from many nations. Whatever its past dreams may have been, it was now a tourist town.

Every time David comes to the turn-off to Port Douglas, he has a feeling of something akin to melancholy. The north is so beautiful and heavy in its strangeness; that road to the resort town seems to David an imposition of humanity's whims upon the land. A place where people had decided to wrestle and wrench the land into servitude for themselves. Maybe that's a good thing sometimes, thinks David, because he likes a good coffee just as much as the next person, and the port is full of good coffee. He'd like one now and he wants to pick up some supplies from the well-stocked supermarket he remembers from the last time he was there.

It is different when it comes to farms, though, he thinks. In contrast to the commercial developments, the agricultural economy here seems more in keeping with the natural habitat, though David knows it is probably doing just as much damage; the landscape hasn't always consisted of sugar cane and banana plantations.

He slows down and indicates that he's turning. Then he stops; he's alone on the road and he stares into the darkness that leads to the comfort of the town.

'Why,' he suddenly asks himself out loud, 'am I here?'

The dark road in front of him doesn't answer.

David thinks again of the town's creator. He can't quite explain why he always feels a twinge of sympathy for Christopher Skase, with his ridiculously long cigars and his Spanish villa, thousands of miles from the town he built. David wonders whether at some point in Skase's exile – perhaps after he really did fall sick – he had ever heard, even if only in his imagination, the lonesome night-cry of a curlew.

David turns the indicator off and slowly, without really knowing why, he drives away from the port and follows the road that leads inland.

At the north and west turn-offs, there are two roads, one leading to the tip of the country, Cape York, the other across the country to the empty triangle inside the top of Queensland. There's a petrol station on the northern highway and David stops for some snacks, water and a newspaper, before driving on north through the canefields until he turns off onto a side road, heading east, back towards the coast.

He makes his way in his whining Tarago to the area within cooee of where the bird was reportedly sighted and pulls up at the side of the road before the gravel turns into a track and becomes too difficult for his cream-bun submarine to navigate. It's completely dark now, the moonlight giving shape to the trees on the horizon in places, leaving other areas pitch black.

He gets out of the car and stretches. It is quiet, unpeopled. He can smell the sea, the mudflats nearby. He hears bush curlews. There are almost as many names for these birds as there are legends: bush thick-knee curlew, bush stone curlew, weelo, willaroo. Depending on the mood you are in, the bird's call can sound like a crying baby or someone giving a long mournful wail.

According to Tiwi Island legend, Bima, the mother of Parukapoli, was tempted by the handsome Japara to leave her son and journey deep into the forest. The boy died from exposure. Later, when his father, Mundungkala, returned from whatever it was he had been doing, he struck Bima on the head with a throwing stick and banished her to the forest. Even though Japara said he could revive the boy, the father refused and carried his child's body into the sea. Before this, there was no death in the world, but now Mundungkala, in his grief and rage, condemned all living things to die. To save his immortality, Japara became the moon, but even so he dies three days a month. Bima was turned into a curlew, whose mournful cries are still heard today. Whether she cries for the death of her son, the loss of her husband or even for her own fate, nobody knows; perhaps she cries for all those things.

David hears the curlew cry again. It's just a story, he reminds himself, and yet standing there beneath the moon he feels faintly uneasy, a sense of no longer existing physically, of approaching death. He would hate not to hear that curlew call, he thinks, for even though he feels unease at the sound, it's not fear. That unease keeps you honest, makes you remember that we all have a certain amount of time here. Has he spent his time here well? he wonders.

He feels the usual strangeness descend on him, his love–hate relationship with being alone in the wild, in the bush. At its worst, he feels vulnerabe – not to the isolation or to the residents of the bush, but to the people who go there to hide.

He opens his fly and urinates, wanting to stay close to the car.

A sudden pale blur crosses the copse of trees silhouetted before him. An owl? He zips up and edges back to the Tarago, keeping an eye on where the bird landed, fumbles around in his swag for his torch and binoculars and then moves stealthily towards the trees. He can still see a patch of paleness through the viewfinder; he waits until he has a sharper focus then flicks on his torch. The beam flashes about momentarily before illuminating the bird. A masked owl. It stares at him as David stares at it. True to the clichés it appears wise, knowing. Unhurried, dignified, it looks around and back at him, or the source of the light. And it is off, David's torch finding then losing the bird's powerful wing beats that make a wondrous ghostly stroke against the tree trunks. Then it's gone.

David uses the torchlight to look around, but is unnerved by the darkness that surrounds him. He slaps away a mosquito and quickly gets back into the cream-bun submarine, where he sprays himself with insect repellent. Then, to his surprise, given the car's vast interior, he fails to find a way to stretch himself out for the night.

There should be more space in a car this size, he thinks. He manages to push the second row of seats back to make more space for the front ones to fully recline. Having done this, he half-lies, half-sits, as though trapped in a dentist's chair, a sensation that makes him feel even more uneasy than when preoccupied with his own mortality.

He lies back, looking at the roof of the car, and thinks about the curlew legend. Why did Bima leave her son? Japara must have been quite charming. It was never explained what Mundungkala had been doing when he went away, and David thinks it a bit rich of him to get so angry that now everybody has to suffer. He supposes he shouldn't get too literal about a legend created to explain why a bird's call sounds so similar to a human's cries, but it does seem as though Bima got the rough end of the deal.

He closes his eyes. Why do legends, myths and religious stories have to be so traumatic, so sad? They almost always deal with some form of treachery or lust or tragedy. If he ever finds somebody to fall in love with, he hopes deeply that it'll be a myth- and drama-free zone.

He thinks about Genevieve Forti, wondering if she is having her dinner tonight with her friends. The ending of their relationship wasn't as fraught as Bima and Mundungkala's. David thinks it wouldn't make a very good myth at all, even if you were to write in a bit of dramatic tension: *Slightly odd man leaves nice woman to see a bird at the top end of the country.*

Hardly explains anything about the human condition, he thinks. But then perhaps Mundungkala too had been off birdwatching? Genevieve is lovely but David isn't that sad. She probably isn't even that sad, either. She wouldn't have wanted to drag the rest of humanity into her dramas like Mundungkala.

Lying there in the Tarago, David can still hear the curlew calling, despite the car's closed doors and windows muffling it slightly.

He feels a stab of sadness; he would like to have somebody feel something for him, care about him, someone to share his 'certain amount of time' with. He opens his eyes. He has never felt like that about anyone. He nods at the realisation, yawns and drifts off to sleep in his dentist's chair.

CHAPTER SEVEN

The dawn comes with the stars seeming to fade to grey, then some colour comes to push the grey away. The birds sing it in. David gets out of the car and stretches, legs numb, neck cricked, staggering as his cramped limbs fail him. While he tries to bring his body to order, he notes the different birds' songs.

He walks down towards the mudflats. The tide is out, the mudflats stretch a long way into an indefinite distant line. Each rivulet, puddle and stain left by the high tide is lit in gentle pinks and oranges, which grow in intensity until eclipsed by the fireball of the sun.

David loves waders. They are still only silhouettes against the brightening sky, but even without detail and with little sound, their movements and shapes tell him plenty. Dotterels running fast and low in the foreground; run, stop, run, stop. He'll have to wait for some more light to be sure which species they are. The long curved beaks of the curlews and whimbrels can be seen on larger birds further out. He sees an eastern curlew, distinguishable by its curving bill – the longest of the waders' at nearly the same size as the bird's body. He can pick out a skulking night heron, low and dark – a shadow rather than a body; a white-faced heron; egrets, great and small; a spoonbill, swishing its bill back and forth through the shallows. One is standing still until *bam*, it spears its beak into a small fish and flies away.

Further out to sea, gulls are on the move, along with some gannets – or perhaps boobies. One of them is preparing to dive, its yellow wing tips catching the orange-gold of the horizon.

David's a satisfied man. This is the life, he thinks. He walks quietly through the mangroves and the shallow water, trying not to disturb anything, pausing frequently to let the birds forget he is there, an invader in their daily routines.

Squatting behind some bushes, hoping for the return of an azure kingfisher, a little surprise of jewel colours among the grey greens of the early morning light, he pulls out his phone, but realises he has no coverage.

What to do? There may be some beautiful birds here, but so far there's no pale pygmy. He only has until tomorrow to see it. The bird may venture elsewhere during the day, but it's likely to return to the same nesting place each night. Should he wait here, do another lap of scanning? Or is the bird just around the corner on the next beach? He'd have to drive.

The kingfisher flies back in suddenly and David is lost in the thrill of being so close to such a northern bird, a tropical bird, almost here in front of him at the time when he should be back in Melbourne, getting on the tram to go to work. The kingfisher darts away again and David stands and stretches.

David can see, vaguely, what looks like human activity maybe a kilometre away; the sunlight glints on something metallic, a closing car door, perhaps. He wanders back to see if these are birders and whether they've had any luck.

Five people are standing around or getting out of their cars. The binoculars, telescopes and cameras that hang from their necks and their multi-pocketed pants and jackets in neutral beiges and greens give them away as birders. David approaches two men who are standing together.

'Hi. Nice morning.'

'Yeah, good,' the older of the two replies.

'Seen anything of note?' asks the younger man.

David shrugs, noncommittal. 'Some beautiful birds . . .' he begins, treading warily, not sure how much to say. 'You guys from around here?'

'Cairns. Cairns bird observers. I'm Ron Bradley,' says the older man. 'This is Pete Dorrige.'

'David Thomas,' David responds, and shakes their hands. 'Nice to meet you. I'm up from Melbourne. This a regular bird outing or a special?'

Ron and Pete steal a glance at each other.

David pulls his only card. 'I'm a friend of Neil's – Neil Murphy. He called me, thought maybe a pale pygmy magpie goose had been spotted.'

Pete and Ron are all cosy and gossipy suddenly, like a pair of galahs who bob and duck, watchful for threats until they decide the danger has passed, whereupon they sway to and fro and chatter.

'It was here the day before yesterday, apparently, then yesterday morning . . .' Ron continues. 'But not last night. A woman up near Wonga Beach said she heard its song – but she's unreliable. Big-noting; done it before. Wants to be a bit of a name.'

'So nothing here this morning?' David asks forlornly.

The older man shakes his head. 'Not so far.'

Pete looks to Ron. 'Maybe we should have gone to Sykes Point?'

'Well, it was Helen who insisted on here.'

One of the birders further down the flats gives a wave and a low call, interrupting what sounds like the beginnings of a well-trodden conversational route between Ron and Pete.

A group is a group, thinks David, as he follows the pair down towards the woman waving. Someone will nearly always be talked about. There will always be a couple or perhaps three people who'll sit and whisper among themselves, perhaps start up a variation on one of the conversational themes. And there will always be one who hangs back and tries to lie low, to sneak under the radar. Gathered together, they form a group.

The trick with groups, thinks David, is to know where to fit in, what role to play.

The six of them stand almost in a row in order to avoid obstructing each other's view, legs strong, binoculars up, looking at where the woman has pointed out a group of waders – bar-tailed godwits. Large waders, a few of them smaller than the others. Probably males, thinks David; much smaller than the females.

'There, just beyond the godwits!' exclaims the woman.

David looks at her. He recognises her, knows it is Helen. She is older than anyone else in the group, perhaps in her seventies. She fiddles with her ear, adjusting a hearing aid, he realises.

'Are you sure it's not just a cotton pygmy goose?' he asks. 'I heard it call, but I can't quite get a fix on the markings . . .'

Helen turns to David. She has accepted him into the group without hesitation but he sees that she doesn't remember him. 'The pale pygmy has a different call and the markings are different on the wing, too,' she explains. 'The immature male differs from the mature in the markings near the eye.'

David puts up his glasses, nodding. He already knows, and has seen this bird, the pale pygmy, before, but loves local knowledge and has a soft spot for the older birdos, who constitute the majority of members of the various clubs and who contribute the most to the volunteer bird surveys. These people, who come from backgrounds almost as diverse as the number of birds they strive to find, identify and catalogue, often widen their interest into land care, weed removal and native revegetation, botanic gardens, volunteering and fundraising. What's not to like, to respect?

'There!' Helen says in a loud whisper.

He remembers her loudness. She probably thinks she's being quiet. Ron and Pete and another woman wince a bit at her noise.

'Hear the call?' she pushes.

David has heard nothing. His stomach sinks a little.

Helen imitates the different notes. *'Dee-dee, dee-dee!*
There, again!'

David strains to hear; nothing.

Ron nods. 'You're right, Helen. If we can just get the
markings . . . Look, he's turning, and we'll get some light
on him . . .'

The bird turns and the sunlight illuminates its head,
clearly showing the lack of telltale markings distinctive to
the rarer bird. But still, a cotton pygmy goose is a good
bird and a sighting worth celebrating.

The birdos look their fill and then exchange a few grins
and grandpa-style high fives, a little uncertain about the
action, but still happy.

They ape their grandchildren, David thinks.

'That's new on your life list, isn't it, Nadia?' says Helen.

Nadia nods, beaming.

David smiles at her, happy, and then focuses his binoculars back on the bird. It opens its beak, calls. David hears
nothing. What else hasn't he heard?

He asks Ron quietly, 'Did the sighting of the PPMG
include the call?'

Ron nods, then says, 'Well, who can tell? Its song is
like nothing else.'

'Hang on there,' says Pete. 'It can sound similar to a
cotton pygmy when it lands if you haven't heard it before.

It's got a longer base note and often calls as it's landing.'
He pauses. 'Well, apparently.'

Ron adds, 'So they say.'

'Yes, so they say,' echoes Pete.

'Have you ever heard it?' asks David.

Ron laughs.

Pete smiles. 'No, never have.'

The little group laughs as one.

'Me neither,' says Ron. 'Not sure who it would have been calling to, here on its own. I suppose it was blown off course. There have been more sightings up at the Cape – it might become endemic.'

'Might do, who can tell?' says Nadia. 'But now I've seen a cotton pygmy. Their numbers are falling in Australia, you know.' And she is smiling.

That's a funny thing to be happy about, thinks David, though he understands Nadia's reaction. The larger Australian species of the cotton pygmy *is* diminishing, although it's not yet threatened, so a chance sighting becomes even more important for the birdos.

'Steady on, Nadia,' says Helen, echoing David's thoughts. 'You shouldn't be happy that there are fewer of something – you sound like somebody who's just bought a painting and then found out the artist has died.'

'And that his name's van Gogh,' says Pete.

'Well now, I'd hardly put a cotton pygmy in the van Gogh!' Nadia retorts.

David hears a rare yet familiar bird call.

The group turns to see Don Barrellon. He stands before them, immense and festooned with bits of twig in his beard and hair. Don must have been banging about in the mangroves, David realises.

'More like a happy little watercolour by Lloyd Rees,' Don says.

'How did you go down in the 'groves?' Ron asks.

'Saw what you did, I think, only I got the arse-end view.'

'Charming!' says Helen. 'You were probably having a smoke, weren't you, Don?'

'Not at all.' He smells of tobacco. 'Well, a true birder knows his bird from one end to the other. Orifice recognition can be very important.' Don knows Helen hasn't heard him.

The two galahs cackle to each other while Don brings his guns to bear on David. 'David Thomas from Melbourne, good to see you got here.'

David nods. Don sounds as if he owns the mudflats they stand on.

'Have you been introduced?' He makes a sweeping gesture towards the small group and bits of mud and twig fly from his big meaty arm.

David indicates he has with a nod to the two galahs.

'Well, this is Nadia Court, Lyndon Pyke and Helen Masters.'

David smiles at each of them and then again at Helen when he sees the flash of recognition on her face. She holds out her hand.

He says loudly, 'We met at Fog Dam.'

'Oh!' she cries.

'On that Darwin trip – you were there with your daughter.'

'Yes, my daughter – she was helping me, being my ears. That's Nadia's job this trip.'

The other birders look to David.

'Fog Dam,' intones Don, and more twigs and mud fly as he waves his arms again for no apparent reason.

'Now there's a beautiful place,' says Helen.

David nods. 'A favourite of mine, too.' He's thinking that he has no one to be his ears. He'll need somebody one day.

Helen pats Nadia on the shoulder and looks at David kindly. 'I can tell you that I didn't hear its call. I was just explaining it to Nads, here.'

Everyone turns back to look at the bird.

'Show us your patterns . . . You blighter!'

David smiles at her use of the word.

Don doesn't miss it either. 'Language, Helen.' He says it loudly for her benefit.

The bird flies away.

Helen sighs. 'Lucky you to be young,' she says to Nadia. 'I can't honestly say I heard it. Lucky I saw it. I didn't hear a thing.' She smiles at David again.

She has a nice smile and warm eyes, he thinks. He nods and looks back out to the bay, suddenly quite embarrassed. She knows, he realises, and he feels unmasked.

The conversation wanders to a few more birds and local news before the birders decide to set off to check the mudflats.

'Where are you staying, David Thomas of Melbourne?' asks Don as the band he has decided he is the leader of begin to walk off.

David shrugs. 'In my car last night.'

The other birders look to Don, as if they expect him to say something to David. Don stares a little and opens his mouth. Nothing comes out. He closes his mouth and thinks some more. 'Then you should give Neil a bell, just to let him know you've made it here.'

David nods. 'Will do.' Helen steps closer. 'You're welcome to join us further down on the flats.'

'Thank you, but I might just push on a bit further up.'

Don crooks his head and suddenly grins. 'David Thomas of Melbourne, Helen, has a knack of just pushing off and finding things. All sorts of things. It's always the quiet ones, you know.'

'Well, Don, you don't have to worry about that then, do you?' she says.

The big man nods to David then gives him a meaty thumbs-up. 'Ring Neil!'

David heads back to his car. He checks his phone; still no coverage. He is dying for a coffee and really hungry, but he can't resist trying the location where the bird was supposedly seen last night. He drives back to the highway and further north, looking for a turn-off.

His phone on the passenger seat lights up: a message. He's back in range. He pulls over and dials. 'Neil. I'm here.'

'David, mate – you're hopeless! Knew you couldn't stay away. Any luck?'

'Nope. Struck out this morning. Saw the greater-girthed Don Barrellon, though.'

Neil laughs.

'Heard anything more?' asks David.

'Nothing firm. He's been here three straight mornings; must have been ten of us to corroborate the song, but no sightings.'

'I heard about the one at Wonga – a bit suspect.'

'She's not always wrong. I might head up there this arvo. I couldn't get away this morning.'

'What'd you think?'

'Who's to know? Might be gone, might hang around for another week. Maybe start at the gorge or the lagoons just behind the village then move down past Cow Bay before dark . . .'

'Sounds like a plan. Neil, what's it sound like – the song?'

'Like nothing I've ever heard.'

'I'd like to hear it.'

'I know, David. I know you would.' A pause, then, 'Enjoy your day in paradise.'

'Thanks, you too.' David hangs up. A day in paradise, he thinks. Well, that has to begin with coffee and food.

The general store in Daintree village sits a hundred metres up the road from the river, in open land. After half an hour of tendrilling roads through the dense rainforest, David is happy to see the sun again.

He orders a coffee and a sandwich, then stocks up on snacks, only noticing the parrot when he dumps the items on the counter.

'Hello,' says David.

The parrot cocks its head to one side and seems to consider the new arrival. David cannot resist the urge to put out his finger, making the bird flap its wings in alarm and jump onto the shop owner's shoulder before flying down the man's open-necked shirt, upside down for a moment, then peeking its head out.

The old man, noticing David's binoculars and reaction to the bird, reacts defensively. 'He's a free bird. I don't keep him in a cage.'

David shrugs. 'I used to have a bird.'

'Talk?'

David takes a moment before he understands the question. 'No, he didn't. He made his wishes known, though.'

'"He made his wishes known"; that's a good one, isn't it, fella?' the man says, addressing the bird, which has gone back down his shirt. 'This one can make his wishes known, too.' The man laughs and looks at the till. 'Twenty-eight bucks'll do it, mate.'

David holds out his debit card. 'Card okay?'

Before the shop owner can take it, the bird reappears and snatches it, flapping its wings and jumping back onto the man's shoulder.

'I'll take that, thank you,' the man says to the parrot, retrieving the card from the bird's beak and using it to give the creature a gentle bop on the head.

David smiles as the shop owner processes the sale, laughter gone and back to business.

He wanders down to the banks of the river to find somewhere in the shade to eat. It's a deep-looking river, judging by its colour; not tempting for a swim, even in the heat. Keeping his binoculars on he watches the birds as he eats. A shining monarch, some Torresian crows, a rufous fantail – that curious and attention-seeking cousin of the willie wagtail – and kingfishers, though none like the tiny azure one he had seen earlier. A blue-winged kookaburra.

Finishing his sandwich, David updates his day list and lies back. A brahminy kite, beautiful with its chestnut-red, white and black colouring, flies high – on the hunt – while above it soar two eagles. Sea eagles or wedgies? David wonders, watching their paths. Wedge-tailed eagles, he decides. The largest of Australia's birds of prey, soaring on the thermals with upturned, fingered wings. David watches them, relaxing, his binoculars now resting on his chest as he lets his mind drift, not asleep, not awake. But finally he drops off.

He suddenly hears a loud voice. He jumps up; a man is yelling, standing next to him. David recognises him as the man from the shop.

'. . . He'll be watching today, that big salty. You here tomorrow? He might watch again, but you won't be here the next day.'

The man is wearing an old army giggle hat. He has a face like an Albert Tucker painting. Grabbing David in his arms and taking him into the death roll, he does a remarkably effective demonstration of a crocodile attack. 'No more naps for you! Want a smoke?'

'No, thanks,' says David.

The man tosses David a bag of sweets. 'You forgot to take your lollies, son.'

'Thanks,' says David. 'No smokes, but would you like a Mintie?'

The man shrugs and then says, 'That'll do; it's moments like this you need a Mintie!'

The two sit in companionable silence for a while, chewing, watching the river flow.

The old man sucks a little on his sweet. 'Lovely lolly, but they always get stuck on me teeth.'

'Hmm,' murmurs David in agreement.

'With fangs like mine that can be a bit of a worry.'

They carry on watching the river for a while and David realises he must have missed something, because the old man is eyeing his binoculars and looking at him expectantly.

'You a birdo?' The man says, pointing to the bins.

David nods.

'Know what you're looking for, then. That goose thing.'

'You haven't seen it, have you?'

'No, but I've seen a fair few people chasing for a look. There've been all types . . .' He sucks on his teeth and picks at something at the back of his mouth before continuing. 'Why do you do it? Why do you lot travel just to look at a bird? I came here years ago, but it was nothing to do with a bird.'

David doesn't say anything.

'Just to mark off a bird in a column in a book? Just a tick or a cross makes you come way up here?'

David looks at him. 'I don't know why myself, sometimes. God knows, it's beyond reason when you really think about it. But I reckon it's about more than just a tick or a cross.'

The man looks at him for a moment and then nods his head. 'Good for you, son, good for you.' He stands up and rolls his tongue over his teeth. 'Just remember, though – no more naps!'

David walks around the clearing and down the road, past a B & B that specialises in catering for birdwatchers. The Daintree forest is home to a huge number of Australia's bird species, so it is on every birder's trip list, as well as those of many tourists. A couple of local birders are among the best in the country, and take tours on the river as well as into the forest.

David went on one of the dawn tours once. He is always one of the youngest on the tours; as a hobbyist, and a weekend one at that, he usually keeps his mouth shut and hides what he knows. There had been international birders on that dawn tour. David isn't sure he could stretch his obsession that far to travel overseas – his interest, yes.

He ponders this now. Would he ever go overseas? There are so many places in Australia, after all, some not yet seen, some begging for a repeat visit. And if he were to venture further afield, where would he go? Here, he could be on a cold high plain, where low trees bow away from the winds and the threat of snow hangs in the air; or on a rolling green hillside, kept luscious by tree-shaded creeks; or in the desert – red desert, salt desert, ancient dreaming desert. Or even here, in the tropical rainforest.

He notices the hard-to-catch gerygones – little birds with quizzical expressions, their red eyes as steady as their movements are rapid. Then a Victoria's riflebird gives him a thrill, its long black tail and shape are a taste of what can be seen in the islands north of Australia. He thinks of jungles and tigers and monkeys, of journeys of imagination and wonder. Yes, he decides, it's more than just a tick or a cross.

CHAPTER EIGHT

Clare walks through the orchard. Or, as her father would say, 'Orchards!' Orchards. The property is split into three distinct growing areas. The bottom orchard is closer to the outbuildings and is the smallest of the three with only about twenty trees remaining. A slow rise leads through a strip of dividing trees that marks the beginning of the middle orchard of about thirty trees and then beyond another dividing line is the top orchard. Here, there are still about forty trees left, mostly in good condition, but she imagines that without anyone to clear, chop and hack it back they will gradually all be swallowed by the forest. She pictures herself with a scythe, arms brown and muscly, back strong, an old hat on her head and the pleasure of a well-earned beer at the end of the working day.

A willie wagtail is flying from tree to tree in front of her, demanding her attention. It flies into an apple tree, boughs hanging low and craggy, and wags its fanned tail vigorously. She wishes she had her camera; it is so close and the blossoms and leaves on the branch would make a pretty picture.

She sees a smaller bird fly through the tree, then another, and another. She tries to keep track of them all, but they flit from tree to tree as soon as she manages to get them in focus. They're small and bright, like coloured-in sparrows, she thinks. Finches. The word comes to her and she marvels at the powers of learning by osmosis; she thought she knew nothing about birds.

She walks beyond the trees and reaches a narrow track leading to a stream that eventually joins the river before plunging down the escarpment in a series of waterfalls which are spectacular in the wet season. Not that you would know now, seeing them in the dry. This country can change quickly. Heavy rain or storm water can fill the dry gully alongside the stream, making small lagoons, and transform the path to the river into a miniature wetlands that can flourish with birdlife.

She looks up into the native trees, not as high at this end of the property but still tall. They dwarf the fruit trees, which were always pruned to allow for picking and to discourage the rowdy bands of cockatoos from sweeping in and devouring the entire crop in an afternoon. Clare can remember Poppa speaking about the birds in the same way he spoke about the local teenagers, describing them as delinquents, vandals, gangs. 'They are hoons! Feathered hoons!' he would exclaim.

Clare laughs at the memory. Her father had wrapped an arm around her grandfather's shoulders and almost sung to him, 'They just love Cirillos' fruits. They're just too sweet!'

'Feathered hoons,' Poppa had repeated.

In the half-dark underneath the canopy of foliage, there is a thick layer of mulched leaves that makes the ground feel soft underfoot. Clare thinks about the spiders and snakes that probably live there. She admits to herself that she is a city girl at heart and smiles at her idea of working through the orchard with a scythe. Do people even use scythes in an orchard? She might well find spiders and snakes in the soft darkness, though, she thinks. She's right about that.

She walks back towards the sunshine. At the end of the track, where it opens into the clearing, lies a dead bird. Clare stares at it. How did she miss it when she was walking in? It lies there, dark and clear against the bright green of the grass. Clare looks around. Has it just died this very minute? Has it fallen from the sky? From a tree?

She's reminded of the way her mother used to talk about Clare's father, who, as a member of the museum society, would keep any interesting birds he found – the dead ones. He'd pick them up, put them carefully into plastic bags and keep them in the freezer until he had a chance to take them to the museum, where they would be stuffed, their details recorded. It was very important to build on knowledge, he would explain to Clare's mother. 'We're as much a part of the web of life as the birds, you know. We need to understand them to understand ourselves,' he would say. 'Of all the animals, people are most like birds – we mate for life, we build our own houses. We nest.'

Clare's mother would nod, before telling Clare, 'Your father's a good man; he doesn't gamble, he brings his wage home, he doesn't flirt with other women – or worse.'

Clare thinks about how much has changed in just one generation – or rather, how little in actuality, but how much in terms of expectations.

Birds had always given her mother the creeps, and after defrosting a tawny owl for dinner by mistake, she finally refused her husband access to the freezer and made him buy one for himself. He called it his 'beer 'n' birds fridge'.

Clare looks at the bird on the ground. Is it rare? Would her dad have kept it? Or would he have let the law of the forest deal with it? What would eat it? Feral foxes? Feral cats?

She touches the body with her foot. It looks uninjured. Was it felled by a sudden heart attack or placed there by an axe murderer to attract Clare's attention, to send her a message? Though she knows she is being ridiculous, Clare can't help but look around, uneasy. It's pretty isolated, no neighbours close by and the birders who arrived last night left at first light – no one would hear her if she screamed. She knows she is taking a city-dweller's suspicions about the country to extremes but feels nervous nevertheless, imagining being followed by a man, his steps quickening; every woman's worst nightmare. Feeling that threat now, here in the country, she longs for men like her father, good men. She knows that not all men are like her father; that's why her mother was always thankful for her Tony, even *with* his love of birds.

Clare feels a mixture of unease and anger at her own apprehension. How can her mind wander so far in an old orchard on a beautiful day? She's about to leave, still thinking about her parents, then turns back and reaches down to pick up the bird with her hat.

She carries the stiff body to the house and places the bird down on the verandah. She goes and washes her hands, then heads to the kitchen, where she inspects the items in the freezer; nothing bird-like there. She looks in the old freezer in the laundry, then further afield in the pickers' huts' fridge; no frozen birds there either. She is relieved.

In the lounge room is an assortment of guidebooks to birds. She reaches for the most straightforward one, *The Slater Field Guide to Australian Birds* by Peter Slater.

She flips through it until she comes to finches. There's a full page of drawings of birds, all perching on a branch in the same profiled position. She recognises none of them as the one she found in the orchard, but she sees the name the Gouldian finch, and remembers her father talking about it. He had said that it was impossibly pretty, almost as if it was wearing a technicolour coat. She thinks of the colours of the Cirillo fruit tins. Her father had always maintained that to see the Gouldian finch in the wild you would have to be very skilful, very patient and very lucky. Clare had asked him once if he had ever seen one and her father had whistled softly, tilted his head and said, 'Well, I'm lucky.' Clare smiles at the memory.

After a good hour of leafing through the pages and poring over the illustrations, she thinks she might have identified the dead bird. It's a finch, she's pretty sure. It isn't coloured like the other birds she saw flitting in and around the trees earlier, yet it shares a similarly shaped little body. The others were redder, perhaps even crimson. Her bird is darker, with a short black bill and a clearly delineated band of black at its throat between a grey head and a pale pinkish-brown body. The overall effect is of a dapper bird, smartly attired for a bit of serious living. She looks at a few more illustrations and decides it's a black-throated finch, before double-checking in another book. This one shows different colours. Perhaps the ink has faded? That could make all the difference. She thinks of some of the art books she had when she was younger, and how startled she was sometimes when she saw one of the actual paintings and the colours were so different.

Clare decides that the bird is definitely a finch. 'You are a black-throated finch,' she tells it when she returns to the verandah. She picks it up and carries it to the copse of trees between the house and the sheds, as far away from the house as possible. She squats, preparing to lay it inside the bushes, where it will be eaten or decompose or succumb to whatever nature wills. She studies its cold, unseeing eyes; its feet, rubbery and bony at the same time; the layers of feathers and the patterns they make; the decisive colours, muted and beautiful. There was something quite marvellous about it in life and now, still, in death. Death. Clare grimaces in both pity and distaste, and then lays it down within the bushes.

Walking back through the trees she tries to think of nothing and just enjoy the warmth and the softness. She closes her eyes. It would be cold in Melbourne, the sort of cold you are sure will never end. She thinks of her small apartment in an old art-deco building, a lovely building but a freezer in the winter.

She has a small platoon of heaters that do the job of warming the rooms for a while, until the old electrical wiring gives up the ghost and short-fuses. It is the sort of apartment that makes people fall in love with the idea of living there, until they experience a Melbourne winter.

Clare stands still. Melbourne is another world away. It is where she lives, where she has made a life for herself, but she knows that things could change easily. People can change. She opens her eyes as a catbird howls like the four-legged animal it is named after. Here in the sun she wonders if she will ever return.

She has taken a year away from her job teaching Humanities at a girls' school. When she told the other teachers that she was leaving, they asked what she would do. Clare had said, 'What else? Write a great book.' They had all laughed together.

There was always a teacher breaking out and wanting to write something instead of teaching by rote books that were both great and ordinary, by authors old and new.

Humanities – what a thing to teach. Some of her brighter students called it 'Inanities' and she had laughed with them. Her students, teenage girls – whole classes of them – sitting there before her.

In some families the teacher is considered to be a kind of third parent, expected to do everything from the tough stuff like reading the riot act, to being a finishing-school expert – a mix between the drill sergeant from *Full Metal Jacket* and *My Fair Lady*'s Professor Henry Higgins. Some parents think the teacher is the root of all their child's problems – a slacker, a nine-to-three-o'clocker who doesn't inspire and doesn't want to.

As for the kids, who knows what students bring with them into class? The stories behind the faces looking at the teacher run across all states of the human condition. Twenty-five, maybe thirty young people sitting before you, ready to listen, to zone out, to take you on and goodness knows what else.

To most students Clare knows she was just somebody who shared a year or two of their lives, somebody who would talk to them about history and novels and ideas that they had to sit through to survive the day. And Clare had always been fine with that. Had she been any different, after all? Not really.

But there is always one student. Always. There was one girl, a bright girl, who had never said much in class but would listen. She had asked awkwardly if Clare would return.

Clare had shrugged a little. 'Who knows?'

The next day the girl had stayed behind after a particularly excruciating lesson about *Romeo and Juliet*. She stood alone at her seat by a window and then quickly walked to where Clare was collecting her things.

'Yes?' said Clare.

The girl blushed and thrust a piece of paper and a packet of chocolates at her. If only this girl had known just how awkward this was for someone like Clare. The poor girl had no idea really who Clare was or what she had lived through.

Clare took the note and read it. In the girl's very neat handwriting and with some accompanying illustrations of flowers and a Batman symbol was the poem 'A Sorcerer Bids Farewell to Seem' by Sylvia Plath.

Sylvia Plath. Oh God, thought Clare.

The girl stood and stared.

'Sylvia Plath?' said Clare.

The girl blushed further and Clare nodded. She was going to leave it there but she couldn't help herself.

'I remember lying in bed when I was, I don't know, maybe fifteen, and thinking that if nothing else, like nothing, was worth living for, and I really felt like killing myself, then I should always remember how much I loved a hamburger. And I'd put myself to sleep thinking of the best things about a hamburger. The bite of everything together, or picking it apart, the onions softened by the sauce, the bread – and it was real bread rolls then, not these sweet buns —'

The girl stared.

'Yes, you probably assume that someone like me thinks everything modern is crap. I know – I'm the sort who hates

McDonald's, Nando's and T-shirts with brands on them. But I don't hate everything modern, only the crap stuff. I mean, paying to be an ad for a company by walking around with their name all over you. And it looks expensive but it's made in China by slave labour . . .' Clare trails off. Now she's blushing almost as much as the girl.

And the girl finally speaks. 'Did you really think of killing yourself?'

Clare freezes momentarily, then carries on while inside she feels a wave of regret at her words, what they may have done, how much she may have revealed or even unlocked in this quiet clever girl.

'Of course not. I just used to wonder how other people could do it when there were so many wonderful things in the world.' She can't stop herself. 'It doesn't have to be hamburgers – it could be the colour of grass or something you like to do. Some music you can listen to. A bike ride. Sunshine . . .' Clare's voice peters out then carries on. 'Or a box of chocolate. Sylvia could have enjoyed chocolate a bit more.'

The girl frowned a little and asked, 'Why? Why should Sylvia Plat have enjoyed chocolate more?'

'Plath.'

'Plath.'

'Do you know anything about Sylvia Plath, Carmel?'

Carmel shook her head. 'I just typed "farewell" and "poem" into a search engine and this came up.' The girl indicated the poem with a small gesture with her finger.

Clare slowly nodded and cursed herself. 'Well she was a very fine poet who had a bit of bad luck but was definitely somebody who could have thought more about hamburgers and chocolate.'

Carmel slowly said, 'Yes, Miss,' unconvincingly, and walked towards the door. She stopped and then turned back, and smiled beautifully. 'I love hamburgers, Miss. Goodbye.'

Clare stands in the orchard now and thinks it would be lovely if more teenagers were like Carmel. Then she takes a deep breath and exhales, saying, 'Sorry, Sylvia,' very softly, before walking back to the house.

Clare sits at the kitchen table eating a sandwich and, only half-interested, sorts through some piles of paper that, though shoved to one end, still take up much of the tabletop. She puts bills in one pile, paper rubbish in another – envelopes, junk mail, old newspapers. Magazines she stacks separately, correspondence goes in yet another pile. She finds a note written on the back of an old envelope. *Tony, thanks for the help last week. Still crook, but working!*

Followed by an indecipherable squiggle. She puts it on the correspondence pile.

There is a copy of a letter her father sent to the Queensland Parks and Wildlife Service. It is about cassowary corridors in new housing estates and the duty of care that householders, developers and government departments have in providing for the endangered birds. He was trying to be formal, thinks Clare, expressing his points in a way that would make the people who decide things take note.

She studies his handwriting. For Clare it belongs on birthday cards and on a present IOU to give her a pair of her team's footy socks, unavailable outside of footy season. On shopping lists and the family budget. It belongs on a card saying, simply, *Love, Dad.*

Realising she needs to keep going with the house-sorting, Clare walks into the lounge room. There are teetering piles of books everywhere, in addition to the hundreds more that fill the bookcases. She tackles one of the shelves, creating new piles on the floor: birds, nature, Italy, classical literature – things she might like to read and keep for herself and an op-shop pile, for books beneath the interest of a second-hand bookseller, comprising ratty copies and 'oncers', books she thinks no one would read twice, the ones where you can never forget who the murderer was once you've reread the first paragraph.

As well as looking at the book titles, she checks inside any books that belonged to her father. A guide to local flora and fauna has the Latin names added alongside the common ones, printed carefully and, Clare suspects, proudly in his young handwriting.

Then she finds an edition of *Goldfinger* by Ian Fleming. She rolls her eyes. Men, she thinks. It seems to be an early edition. A drawing of a man she supposes is James Bond adorns the cover, though he looks more like an ABC weatherman from the 1970s than a secret agent. She wonders what interest her father had in the adventures of the ABC weatherman/womanising super spy. She can't remember him talking about this novel or anything like it; she can only remember him reading poetry and science and bird books. Maybe this was just escapism? The cover is almost like one of the fruit tins – not as beautiful but certainly of its time.

She decides to keep it if there is any trace of her father within its pages – his name, perhaps, or a message from whoever gave it to him. She flips to the title page and finds nothing, then carries on leafing through. She stops at some notations in her father's hand, looks more closely at them and then bursts out laughing. They are golf scores between Goldfinger and Bond. Her father had made hole-by-hole notes of what was happening in the story: *First hole, par 5, Bond one over (6) and Goldfinger one under (4).* He had followed the characters' scores right until the end of the game. *Bravo, Bond!* is just legible in tiny letters to indicate that the super-spy weatherman had won, but it had been crossed out and down the side of the page is written, *Well played, mate. Well done, Jim.* Clare reads it again and wonders whether he had been practising his English. Or rather his Australian.

She flicks through, past the golf game, and finds more handwriting. *Pazzo. L'inglese! Funi, funi, funi!* And an accompanying translation: *Crazy! Silly Pommy bastard!*

Then, on the back page in capital letters is written, *Picnic Reads!* The ink there hasn't really faded, the hand a little unsteady but still clear. Picnic Reads? Clare puts the book on a new pile, then goes back through the other piles she has been making, pulling out anything remotely personalised and adding it to this new pile.

Deciding to take a break, she leaves the lounge room to begin her coffee-making routine. In the kitchen there are also some piles, one cupboard begun then abandoned.

Picnic appears at the doorway, standing like a statue on the other side of the screen door, an eye on Clare.

'Hello there, Picnic,' says Clare. 'Can I get something for you?'

The bird is motionless.

Clare pours her coffee and goes to the door to take it out onto the verandah. The bird is blocking her way.

'Are you going to let me out?' Clare pushes the door gently.

Picnic only moves far enough to let Clare out, the screen door closing behind her with a familiar squeak, bang and click.

Clare looks back. Picnic doesn't budge from her position. 'You're a cool customer, aren't you?'

Instead of her usual perch on the edge of the verandah Clare sits in the chair she remembers her father sitting in, and her grandfather before him. Picnic stands to attention. Clare looks at her. 'What?'

Picnic looks back.

Clare holds her hand out to the bird. Picnic doesn't move until Clare is nearly touching her, and then takes a step back.

'No pats, then? Fair enough.' Clare looks at the bird for a while and then says matter-of-factly, 'You don't actually look very cuddly. Nothing personal, just the warm-puppy factor is a bit . . . well, missing in you.'

The bird turns its head to one side, then back to Clare.

'As for this tail-wagging, I've got a vague idea of what mood you're in, but I have to guess a bit here, Picnic.'

The bird stares at her.

'You're not going to give me anything, are you? Can you wink?' Clare sips at her coffee.

The bird follows her movement with its head.

'Surely you don't want a cup of coffee?' The bird cocks its head the other way and looks at her.

Clare thinks. What is it that goes with a coffee? A biscuit. Dad would have had a biscuit, wouldn't he? She tries to remember. She can't possibly be losing sight of her father; it's only been a matter of weeks. She imagines morning tea, a morning coffee. He'd be sitting out here, sometimes resting his feet on the large wooden trunk he kept to one side of a small table.

She thinks for a minute and decides to open the trunk. Inside is a collection of books – poetry, science, some stories about birds, a copy of *The Snow Goose* by Paul Gallico, and some histories. She picks up an anthology of poems devoted to birds. There on the title page are the handwritten words *Picnic Read*s.

Clare looks at the bird. 'Did he used to *read* to you, Picnic?'

The bird stares back.

She is beginning to understand her father's home-alone routine. 'He read to you – when he was alone here. Biscuits and books!' she exclaims.

Clare gets up and goes back into the kitchen to the pantry. If there are any here they might be a bit stale, she thinks.

Biscuit tins, recognisable from her childhood, line the shelves, but the tins' contents have long since ceased to reflect their branding. A strange child with painfully tight pigtails, pale blue eyes and a terrified-looking spaniel decorate one that now contains rice, the flour tin has a castle on it, and a Colosseum-adorned tin contains rubber bands and bits of string.

Among them Clare finds a Rawleigh's tin. When she shakes it it rattles – perhaps tacks or pins have found their way into this part of the pantry. And then she sees the sweet-biscuit tin covered in blue and green water lilies, looking as old as Monet would be now. She lifts the lid. Yes! She has found the biscuits – some loose, others in unopened packets. There are ginger nuts and Iced VoVos. Clare shakes her head, smiling. They must have stopped making those years ago, she thinks, probably even when Arnott's was still an Australian company.

She looks around and then as she sees it she remembers; the savoury biscuits were always kept in a rectangular yellow Tupperware container with a gone-to-grey-white lid with a burn mark on one corner. Inside are Jatz and Vita-Weats, just as she remembers. She takes a couple of each and heads back out to the verandah.

CHAPTER NINE

Clare sits at her father's desk and picks up the handset of the old telephone. Fixed to one wall by the desk are pinboards, each covered in random notes and instructions: a shopping list, a reminder to check brain-scan results, a World War Two ration card.

She looks at them as she dials her brother's number. Brain-scan results? She is wondering what this might mean when the phone is answered and she can hear the sounds of breakfast and kids getting ready for school.

Her niece answers, '*Allo?*'

'*Bonjour, Juliette. C'est tante Clare ici.*'

'*Papa, c'est tante Clare,*' the little girl calls out.

Clare hears her brother shouting in the background, '*En anglais, Juliette. Tante Clare ne parle pas français.*'

'Hi, Auntie Clare,' Juliette answers. 'How is Australia?'

'*Je – J'ai vu un wallaby aujourd'hui – un petit kangaroo.*'

'Really? Really? In Melbourne? On a tram?'

For heaven's sake, thinks Clare, her niece's English is perfect and she's only five! She sighs, defeated, and reverts to English. 'No, I'm at Poppa's house in North Queensland. Remember you came here once? We saw the crocodile . . .'

'Did you see a crocodile yet? Can I come?'

'Yes, I would love you to come.'

'I have to go to school.'

'Oh. That makes it tricky.'

There is a pause, then, 'Here is Papa.'

Ollie comes on the line. 'Hi, Bear. I hope you weren't trying to talk French to your niece?'

'Oh, thanks!'

'Don't worry – I can't keep up with her either. You're just a convenient excuse when she sounds too Australian at school.'

This was Ollie being smart. There is a silence, then, 'Hey, how are you?' he asks.

'I'm at Dad's.'

'Yeah?'

'There's a bunch of birding people who've come to stay for a day or two in those sheds.'

'You mean the lodges?' Ollie says, sounding a little poncy to Clare. 'I thought I told people they were closed?'

'You did, but apparently there is some bird that is a bit of an event so they have come up to see it. Some of them knew Dad, apparently.'

'Yeah?'

'Well, that's what Murph said.'

There is a pause and then a laugh. 'Christ!'

He is admonished by one of his daughters in the background, but she is giggling as she speaks.

'*Bon, je suis désolé*,' says Ollie. 'You mean Murph the smurf?'

'One and the same; he came over yesterday. I didn't recognise him at first,' Clare says. 'He was at Dad's funeral but neither of us recognised him.'

'Well, it's been a while, Bear.'

'Certainly has, Ollie Dolly.' Hearing her brother's intake of breath, Clare smiles.

'Yeah, well . . .'

'You are such a sook, Ollie.'

'How long are they staying?'

'Not long – a day or two, like I said. They're not much trouble – came in late last night and were all out at first light, well before I was up.'

'Are you charging them anything?'

'Well, that doesn't seem fair, really. I haven't been put out at all, they've made all the beds and made the place tidier than it was when they arrived.'

'Is that why you rang? To let me know? It's okay, Bear.'

Clare doesn't say anything; she can hear chaos at the other end of the line, kids' laughter and some yelling. None of it angry, just early morning noise.

'It sort of feels right that they're here, Ollie. I know it sounds dumb but . . . I don't know.'

'What do you want me to say, Clare?'

She bristles; suddenly she's not 'Bear' anymore. 'I don't want you to feel you have to say anything – *Oliver.*'

'Yes you do. You want me to say, "Hey, maybe you could stay there?"'

She doesn't respond.

Ollie puts on a younger-brother voice. 'Hey, Clare, maybe you could stay there, at Dad and Poppa's old place in Far North Queensland.'

'Yeah . . .' she says slowly. 'I'm at the "bird house" and it's like I . . . I know nothing about birds. Well, not *nothing*, no. They fly.'

'Not all of them.'

'That would be supporting my point. Although I did come across a black-throated finch this morning.'

'Well, that must have been pleasant for you.'

'It was dead.'

'Maybe not so pleasant for the black-throated thing, then.'

'Finch.'

'Yes, the finch thing.' There's a short silence before Ollie goes on. 'Cla-are . . .' he says, drawing out her name and ending with an upward inflection that makes him sound very Australian. No smooth Oliver Cirillo, international lawyer, now, she thinks, smiling.

'Clare,' he repeats, in his international-lawyer voice this time. He must have heard himself, Clare decides. 'You hate people. You once said your idea of hell would be to run a B & B and, if I recall, purgatory to stay at one.'

Clare, defeated, nevertheless perseveres. 'I could make it bigger – employ other people to do the bits I don't like . . .'

'Bird World. We'd have to get some rollercoasters.'

'And a water slide.'

'And a "Big Bird", like the Big Pineapple.'

'And crocodiles – we'd need an enclosure.'

'Of course – crocodiles! Juliette would like that. She would insist, wouldn't you, Juliette?'

'*Oui, oui – crocodiles, un bon nombre de crocodiles,*' Clare hears her niece say.

'And we could sell bird statues,' Clare continues.

'Indigenous birds. Toss out your flamingos and storks. We could have bird burgers. Kingfisher crisps.' Ollie becomes distracted, his voice muffled. '*Un minute, Clara. Je parle à tante Clare.*'

'*Ma tante Clare! Ma tante Clare!*'

Ollie returns to the phone. 'She loves her old namesake.'

Clare corrects him lightly, though flattered. 'Her not-so-old namesake loves her, too.'

Ollie breathes out deeply. 'Sell it, Clare. There isn't any part of running a B & B you'd like. You'd spend the whole time under the bed being grumpy.'

'Would Dad hate me?'

'Dad didn't always do what Grandpa wanted.'

'I know.' She's deliberating about how open she can be, how honest. 'It's not like I've got much else, Ollie, and I can do bits of work from here. Do we really need the money? I mean, what's money? It's not really important.'

'Oh Christ, Clare! It's "not important", is it?' Ollie is incredulous. 'It's the stuff you pay the rent with. Or put in the bank.'

'Maybe I could stay up here and write a book . . .'

'The old "great Australian novel"?'

'That's the one.' She pauses. 'Or we could do what Grandpa wanted – keep the orchard going. You could come back and run the business. The kids would love it. We loved it when we were kids.'

'And you can write the marketing copy. Quick, how many words rhyme with "pecans"?' says Ollie.

It was a game they would play in the back seat of the car as children on family road trips up and down the coast.

'Flan, can . . .' Ollie begins.

'Come on: pee-eecan,' encourages Clare.

'The Ghan, chimpan-zee, umm . . . Japan. Christ. I'm still crap at it. Shall we go on to custard apples?'

'No thanks, unless you're paying the phone bill now.'

'Clare, I'm a lawyer; I never pay. And you're forgetting the wet season.'

'I know. How's Isabelle?'

'Good, she's good. She's blowing you a kiss right now. We're all good. The kids loved their presents from Australia. Juliette is obsessed with crocodiles. They fit right in with the dinosaurs. Any animals, really. Anything that has a small plastic version that's sharp and vacuum-cleaner-wreckable. *Petite* Clara walks around with the diamond python like it's a feather boa and she's at the fair.'

'I know – it's mad. It's just hard when I'm here. And it's cold in Melbourne.'

'You wouldn't seriously think about it, Clare?'

There's a long pause. 'Well, it's not like anyone wants me anywhere else.'

Ollie sighs.

'Ollie, there's so much of Dad here. Of stuff I remember . . .'

'You have hundreds of friends.'

'Don't be patronising. You just want the money.'

'Hang on a sec, Clare, get off your high horse. You want the money, too. What am I supposed to do, just say, "Oh no, I don't need that money, you keep it to have a nice holiday house for the winters"?'

'It could be your holiday house, too.'

'Without any money, Clare, I wouldn't be able to get there. I didn't ask you to clean it up; you don't have to do this. If you're finding it too hard, just lock up and leave.' Her brother's tone is defensive and meaner than before.

Another pause, then, 'Look, I've got to drop the kids at school and get to work. Speak to you soon.'

There's a click and the sounds of a full and busy life cut out, leaving Clare feeling deaf as she tries to readjust to the less chaotic sounds of her own surroundings: the birdsong of nightfall, Picnic giving one of her haunting calls. Though there is no echo, the last plaintive note seems to hang in the air.

Clare has a sip of her wine, and then calls out to Picnic, 'No! No good. No more biscuits!'

Then she walks into the living room to the pile of books where she left *Goldfinger* and opens it: *Picnic Reads*. She smiles and heads back to her chair on the verandah.

CHAPTER TEN

Out on the northern mudflats, David is scanning for the bird. It's not there. He races back to the place where he started this morning. He has spent most of the day driving between the various places where the bird has allegedly been sighted. Now, with light fading rapidly, he continues further towards the mangrove area and leaps out of his car. The sun is sinking lower on the horizon and he knows he's getting into dangerous territory.

Sixty minutes later he says softly, almost to himself, 'A lovely day at the beach.'

'What's that?' says Neil Murphy as he fastens the tow rope to the cream-bun submarine.

'Oh, nothing,' David says, and then remembers himself. 'Look, are you sure you don't want a hand?'

'Jesus, Dave, do you want to rip the other fender off as well?' Neil says, laughing.

'No, I don't think that would be a good idea.' David turns back to face the water. He's seen some good birds – lots of waders, more cotton pygmies – but no goose. Of course, it's hard to be certain in the failing light, but he hasn't heard the call.

At one point he thought he saw it, just briefly, deep in the mangroves at the far end of Wonga Beach. He thought it was the right size and shape: its head and bill were rounded, but he couldn't see the coloured bars at the end of the tail. If he had heard the call then that would have made all the difference. He approached the mangroves cautiously, but then his phone rang – loudly. He had forgotten to put it on vibrate, but it was too late to worry about that.

The birds scattered – not so much from the noise as his reaction to it. He had tripped over his feet and then yelled in frustration, searching each of his many pockets for the phone. Finally locating it, he pulled it out and his wallet fell out onto the muddy ground. As he bent down to pick it up, his binoculars strap hit his forehead.

He thought it might have been Neil Murphy finally ringing him back; David had left three messages. He looked at the screen, and his bins hit his chin. It was Genevieve Forti. 'Great.'

He looked back to where he'd seen the birds, now long gone. Should he answer? A sandfly that had been buzzing about nearby made its presence felt and David jumped up and slapped the back of his neck with the palm of his hand.

It hurt. He made an involuntary groan and then looked down to see he had accidentally pressed 'Answer' on his phone.

'Genevieve.'

'Found your bird?'

'No. No, not yet.'

'Having fun?'

He thought about his day. 'Well, yes.'

'But you haven't found your bird?'

'Thought I did just a moment ago, but . . .'

'But?'

'Well, I don't know.'

Silence. A bird cried.

'What sort was that?'

'A dotterel. A little wader. Pretty bird.'

'David . . .'

'Are you still going to dinner tonight?'

'Yes, I'm looking forward to it. It'll be a lot of fun.'

'I'm sorry.'

Genevieve laughed. 'No, I don't think you are, really, David Thomas, but you know – that's okay.'

'No, I am. Really.'

'Well, maybe you are a little sorry, but even though you haven't seen your bird, you're still happy.'

'Genevieve —'

'Look, David, it's good. I've been thinking since you called to say you were going north – I think I'd like you to be a friend. It would make life much easier.'

David didn't say anything, waiting. Another bird cried. 'That was a tern. Just in case you're wondering.'

'David, as a friend you'll be annoyingly eccentric, but as anything else you'd be a candidate for justifiable homicide.'

'Do you think?'

'No. I just . . . Well, I just think that you're a nice man and I like you and I would like to leave it at that.'

'Genevieve?'

'Yes?'

'You would make a great myth to explain life and then base a faith system on.'

There was a little laugh. 'I'm going to take that as a compliment.'

'I think you should.'

'Well . . .'

'Yes?'

'I hope you find that bird, David. I really do.'

'Thank you.'

'Take care, you mad bugger.'

'You too.'

A bird cried. He was about to identify it for her, but she had hung up.

'It's the dotterel again,' he said softly.

And on the beach, in the mangroves by himself, he felt terribly alone.

He stood feeling like that for some time until another sandfly bit him. He struck his neck, sighed in exasperation at the pain of the bite, the thump he'd given himself, the lack of Rid, and the absence of the goose. He decided he would head to the next beach along and scan the inlet that bordered it at one end.

He'd spent almost an hour there before a text message from Neil Murphy told him to try a small lagoon just behind the next-to-last beach before town. Neil would meet him there.

David made a mad dash to get there before the afternoon completely disappeared. The beach was much busier than Wonga and he drove the whining van as safely as he could through groups of tourists and locals.

He was trying to save time, he later told Neil. That's why he'd gone as far as he could in the big car.

'Sorry, I didn't think you'd have to make a special trip. Thought you were coming up to see the goose. Well, the pygmy goose, not this goose.' David indicates himself.

Neil shrugs. 'I got caught up with something. Things are busy at the moment.'

'With all the birdos up here?'

'Well, that and other stuff. Like —' He stops.

David looks up at him.

'Like stuff,' says Neil, his head tilted to one side.

Then they look at the car. It's seriously bogged and the tide is coming in.

'It's just that I decided to push the envelope a bit.'

'A bit!' Neil assesses the axle, deep in mud. 'Did you actually try and reverse?'

'I sort of got a bit mixed up.'

'Oh yeah?'

'I forgot I was in the equivalent of the community bus and – yeah, you know, which one was drive and which one was reverse . . .' David shakes his head and the sandfly – he is sure it is the same swine of a thing – bites his neck again.

He gives himself another thump, but this time he doesn't react; it is almost second nature now.

This is new to Neil. 'No need to beat yourself up about it, mate.'

'You didn't see what I did to it – the poor car sounded as if it was going to cry.'

Neil laughs.

'Poor old cream-bun sub,' says David, and pats the side of the Tarago.

'I don't suppose you were meant to take it off-road, for insurance and stuff.'

'I didn't get any insurance.'

Neil looks at him.

David gestures ineffectually. 'The guy was wearing a really horrible shirt.'

'That explains it,' says Neil, dryly.

The two men try to pull the van free but after a few promising groans and a bit of movement here and there, it finally gives a trembling shudder, the mud under the tyres makes a farting sound and the rope snaps. Then it shakes itself like a chook about to roost and settles – almost elegantly – back into the mud.

The second time, David attaches the steel-tipped rope to the rear fender. The rope stays intact and attaches to the fender, but unfortunately the fender doesn't completely stay attached to the van. David yells and Neil manages to stop his Land Rover just in time to prevent any more damage.

He gets out and goes back to the van. He measures the fender with his eyes for a while and then gives it a great kick with his Blundstone-covered foot and the fender clicks back into position.

'Like putting a dislocated finger back into place – just look where it goes and shove it back in fast,' he explains.

David nods. He looks down at Neil's fingers and sees that a few of them look like he practises what he preaches.

Neil adds a few finishing tugs to the rope, which he's attached to the front fender this time.

Finally, he goes to the back of his Land Rover and flicks on the winch. This time the van rises, trembles and begins to move.

'I think she likes it, David,' he says.

The mud groans a farewell to the van and the pair guide it up the sandbanks. Then they wander back down to the beach.

'I thought you might have ticked the PPMG this morning. That was why you left all the messages.'

David makes a semi-grimace, a little shake of the head. 'I thought I might have this afternoon, but it was pretty much a silhouette so I couldn't really tell. It didn't call – I wanted to get closer, get a proper visual on it.'

'What happened?'

'I got a phone call, from a . . .' He thinks for a bit. 'From a friend.'

'Some friend!'

'Yeah.' David shrugs his shoulders.

'Has *anybody* seen it?'

'Apparently Barrellon's little group heard the call. It wasn't long after I went to see how they were going; they were all in a bit of a flap. They pointed to where they thought it might be, I went closer to it, but didn't hear or see anything.'

Neil shrugs. 'Bad luck.'

'Do you think it's still about?'

'Well, who knows? It's been a few days since it was heard, it might have scooted off.' He pauses and then goes on, 'They reckon there's some rain on the way.'

David turns and an anguished look falls across his face. 'Rain,' he says, sadly.

'Sorry, mate.'

'*And it was such a lovely day at the beach*,' says David. 'That was the title of a composition test at primary school. We were given grey Department of Education workbooks with the state crest on the cover and illustrations of road safety on the back. In the story I wrote that we helped Mum pack, took our buckets, spades and picnic and sat happily in the back of the car while Dad drove to the sea.'

David pauses. 'Dad always drove in the stories – always sand castles and splashing and us coming home after a lovely day at the beach. The end.

'I spent all day at the beach, Neil, and I didn't take spades, buckets or a picnic. Just took myself – and my notebook.'

'Like all these guys,' he says.

There are still quite a few people on the beach. They've made a day of it all right, David thinks. 'Everyone has their iPads, iPods, mobile this or that, or some other digital device,' he says.

Neil grunts and then says, 'Remember the days when all you took to the beach was a transistor?' He looks at two teenagers, sitting with their heads down and plugged into whatever device was pile-driving noise into their ears.

David winces a little.

'Kids now wouldn't even know what a transistor was,' Neil says.

'I remember my sister being given one that you could clip around your leg,' says David.

'My sister had one of those, too,' says Neil. 'Her boyfriend gave it to her.'

'That was a serious gift.'

Neil nods. 'They were pretty serious – they both used to wear matching-coloured crocheted togs.'

'Well, you'd be hard-pressed to find a kid now who could get their head around crocheted bikinis, let alone transistors!'

'Crochet? Is that what Nanna used to do with coat hangers?' says Neil in his best teenager voice.

'Ah, the seventies.'

'Had an uncle who'd call questionable bathing attire "New Australian togs". He reckoned that only recently arrived immigrants would wear outlandish and outrageous swimming costumes.'

David smiles and waits for what's next.

'You know, mate, my sister's boyfriend was Portuguese.' Neil holds up his hands as if he's just proved a point, no more argument needed. 'Explained the crocheted swimmers.'

David looks around them now, at Australians of so many races. There are some interesting choices of swimwear on display, and in some cases ambition clearly outweighs good sense and taste. The pick is a fellow channelling Daniel Craig's Bond from *Casino Royale*. He wears second-skin aqua shorts over his rather rotund southern Australian non-tanned version of a 007 body.

David and Neil consider this and then hear a call. Well, David half-hears it.

'Bird! Bird!' someone close to the water calls out.

'Look at the bird! The big bird!'

A jabiru has slid from the horizon and is now descending slowly into the shallows not far from the water's edge. Everyone stops to watch, then walks en masse towards the water.

David and Neil stand still and watch, too, until David suddenly notices 007 nearby, holding one of his kids.

'Can you see? See the big bird?' the man says to his daughter. The little girl squeals with delight.

Two teenagers who've been sunbaking sit up, pull out their iPod earphones and point, open-mouthed. The bird simply stands, staring into the water.

One man, who is standing near David, holding his girlfriend's hand, looks, transfixed. 'That is so lovely,' the girlfriend says as the jabiru rises slowly above the water.

It is indeed lovely, David thinks, and even though he hasn't seen *his* bird, there is something about this moment shared with strangers on a beach that makes him realise – or maybe remember – how fine it is simply to *be*.

'A lovely day at the beach. The end,' he says.

CHAPTER ELEVEN

The van only just starts, whining with such misery that heads turn as David drives it away from the beach, following Neil.

After reaching a crossroads they keep going to a petrol station further ahead, where they both pull over. Neil walks back to David's car.

'You'll need fuel and you'll need help with the motor,' he says. 'See if it turns over and sounds better when it's dried out a bit. Don't worry – this bloke is a mate, he should sort it.'

Neil's mate, the mechanic Warren, assures David he can sort it. His skin is dark with grease and oil and dirt, making his bright blue eyes stand out. He cackles like a crow, a large friendly crow, and David can barely understand a word he says. All he can make out is, 'You'll be right, right, yeahhhh, yo'b beeee right. Sorted. Sweet sweet.'

Neil translates for him: according to Warren, the van only needs an engine steam and a new fan brace and muffler bracket. Warren can sort it all out tomorrow. It's best not to drive it tonight as something more serious might happen if David tries to push it too far – better just to leave it in the garage for now. Neil adds reassuringly, 'Don't worry, mate, it takes years to be able to understand what he says, but he'll look after you.'

'Sweet, yeah, sweetmate sweet,' says David in response.

'Where'd you sleep last night?'

David points to the van.

Neil takes in David's size and then looks at the awkward design of the van's interior. 'You would have had a good sleep then.'

'Would've been better if I hadn't run out of Rid in the night.'

'I'd ask you to my house,' Neil says, before pausing.

David raises his eyebrows, intrigued.

'But I can't really ask you.'

David waits.

'To my house,' Neil clarifies, before twisting his face and taking a deep breath.

David prompts, 'I could really use a shower . . .'

'You could.'

'I know.'

There is a silence.

'I got married.'

'You?'

Neil's face is still twisted.

'What?' says David.

Neil breathes out.

'When?'

Neil's face softens. He says nothing.

David looks at him. Neil's like a magpie: watchful, resourceful and totally of this landscape, but territorial.

'Well, that's good news,' says David. 'And it deserves a bit of a celebration. Besides, at the very least you deserve a six-pack for helping me out.'

'Six-pack?'

'I meant a carton.'

Neil smiles. 'Two slabs – and a couple of pizzas. And a family-sized block of chocolate.'

David nods and heads over to the general store beside the servo. Neil calls something that he doesn't hear, but he nods anyway. He goes to the liquor section and is met by Warren the friendly-crow mechanic who is also, it appears, the friendly-crow general-store proprietor. His hands are slightly cleaner now, but his conversation just as indecipherable.

David engages in a baffling discussion with Warren before finally – and triumphantly – emerging with a large cardboard box containing two cartons of XXXX Gold and a bottle of the best champagne that was available, two frozen pizzas and a family-sized block of chocolate.

As he's leaving a teenager walks in, all loose limbs and easy movements, but angry looking. Maybe he's not angry, thinks David. Maybe that's just the way he looks.

Outside the door is a group of about five other young men, milling around underneath a lone streetlight. They are laughing as David emerges from the store and then go quiet when he walks past. Then they laugh again.

Instinctively David wonders if they are laughing at him.

'Bloody hell, David,' says Neil, 'I was joking. You didn't have to get all that stuff.'

The kids laugh again. David looks back and then walks to where Neil is leaning against his Land Rover. 'Well, you know, I'm just a very literal bloke.' They both laugh.

They are quiet while they load up the car, then Neil says, 'Lily.'

'Lily?'

'Yeah, that's my wife's name.'

'So, how long have you been married? How long have

you been together? I didn't know you'd even met someone. Did you have the big white hoo-ha?'

Neil shakes his head quickly. 'Mate, we would have asked you if it were a big deal. We got married in Thailand.'

'Thailand? What were you doing in Thailand?'

Neil is almost defensive now. 'I went there on holiday.'

There is a pause; Neil isn't going to give up information easily and David isn't rude enough to keep pushing him. He turns away, thinking more about himself than Neil. Marriage. That must make him one of the last single guys without some major reason for it. I'm not a junkie or institutionalised, he thinks. Or a priest. He turns back to Neil, who offers a shy smile.

'If it can happen to me, mate, it can happen to anyone.'

'So I guess it'll soon be kids, the works?'

'It already is. Twins.'

'Twins! How could I not know about twins!'

'Oh, well – Lily wanted to have them at home in Thailand with her mum and I had to be here working a lot. I went over for the birth, but had to come back. But we're all together now. It's just . . . it's only been a week and Grandma doesn't speak English and is a bit suspicious of *farang*.'

David looks at him blankly.

'White people. So it's not a great time to have you to stay. It's all still a bit —' Neil wiggles his hand from side to side, 'iffy.'

David thinks for a bit. The teenagers, still standing under the light, laugh again, more loudly. He looks over and sees one of the boys trying to catch a big moth with his hat; when he's caught it, he puts the hat back on his head, trapping the moth. The boy does a crazy dance then turns to his friends. He lifts off his hat, the moth flies away, the crazy dancing stops and he is back to normal. They all howl with laughter.

David looks. Just kids – not angry. Just kids. So often things turn out to be much simpler than they appear.

'Have you told anybody else about your . . . um . . . situation?' David asks.

'No, mate. We'll keep it a secret for a bit . . . Won't we?'

David nods. 'Well, we've all got secrets.'

The kids by the store start to move off. Neil greets one of the boys, who's riding a bike. 'Hey, Aaron, going okay? Catch anything today?'

'Nah. Big croc been eating every bugger fish up Murphys Inlet.'

'Make sure you don't take a nap on the banks of the inlet,' David says.

The kid studies him.

'First day they see you . . .' says David.

'Second day they watch you . . .' says Neil.

'Third day they take you!' yells the kid on the bike.

The two men, leaning against the Land Rover, watch the kids move off. Disappearing into the dark it's hard to believe they had even been here, thinks David. He has an odd feeling of floating unease. It's not fear but the knowledge that everyone is just passing through.

Neil turns to him and says, 'Tony Cirillo.'

David nods.

'You know he died?'

'Yeah, I heard.'

They stand together for a while longer.

'What made you think of Tony?'

'He used to fill up his car here. We'd have a bit of a chat whenever we saw each other,' Neil says. 'It was pretty quick. Heart attack. I keep meaning to send out a special newsletter, but . . .'

'Poor Tony Cirillo,' says David. 'Twins,' he then says sympathetically. 'And an in-law.'

'Yeah, twins,' repeats Neil with no emotion. 'And an in-law.'

They are both quiet.

'Do they really think it's going to rain?'

'They do. Maybe it'll just be overnight.' Neil goes on, 'I don't think the family were into the birds aspect of the property. They actually shut up the lodges. Well, Ollie – the son – did. He was here for the funeral, but lives in Europe somewhere.'

'Poor Tony Cirillo,' repeats David.

'The daughter's there now – she's just come back up to sort the place out. Clare's her name. Knew her when she was a kid – they came to stay during the holidays. Clare.' Neil hesitates, thinking about something, and decides to let it go. 'Clare is just here cleaning up but she opened the lodges up again for Barrellon and Helen and that lot. They're staying a couple of nights.'

He looks at David, who gets the hint. 'Maybe you could drop me there? They should have room. I might as well. I might go there and have a crack at a rainbow pitta before I hit the flats again. Have to see it tomorrow, and get something done with the bloody car. I have to get back.'

'Girlfriend?'

David makes a face. 'Not anymore. Actually, we weren't quite up to that point. A bird trip at this stage usually kills it.'

'Why do you go out with these city girls? Why not find a birder girl?'

'There aren't any younger than sixty. And the single ones are getting closer to eighty.'

'Not true. You just don't want to settle to being a dag like the rest of us. You're an inner-city, latte-drinking greenie that actually votes Liberal because —'

'Go easy, mate.'

'Confess: you would die if you had to wear those pants that zip off into shorts!'

'*You* confess: you like a latte, yourself!'

'Nope, I still like my coffee without milk, mate.'

'Christ. Everything I've done has been this. If I'm no good at birds, if I just can't hear them . . . I'll have to go on a minibus with a guide telling me where to look for the birds. Having some smart-arse eight-year-old pointing out that he can hear the call of the boobook owl. Shit. I've been a guide. Birding was only meant to be a hobby, anyway. It's just got out of hand.'

'Then it doesn't matter if your hearing goes. Your taste buds might improve. You could learn to like your coffee black,' Neil says.

The two men are in no hurry to go. They stand beside the Land Rover, staring at the glow of the streetlight, which has attracted a crowd of insects. A few cars have started arriving; their occupants park, waiting for something. A tradie's ute pulls up and three young men get out and lunge into the store, all yelling. A couple of dogs tethered to the back of the ute's cabin bark in answer to the men's yahoo-ing.

David only hears bits and pieces of what the men are saying to each other. He turns to Neil. 'Please don't tell anyone.'

'What's to tell? Who's there to tell? Anyway, we've all got our secrets.'

A bus pulls in across the road and a few people get off. This crossroads seems to be a major stop, though there is nothing really here except the service station. One road leads up and inland, the other continues along the coast, on to Cape Trib and, eventually, in some sort of dirt-track fashion, all the way to the northern tip of Australia.

A couple of kids in school uniform run across the road from the bus and jump into a waiting four-wheel drive, which immediately turns away with such a familiar ease that David imagines it must do this trip almost daily.

A woman jogs towards another four-wheel drive. She climbs in and it pulls off more sedately and drives into the darkness.

There's one person left. A woman. Young. Maybe only in her late teens. Neil looks over at her. David follows his gaze. They sense something isn't quite right.

The men from the tradie's ute are buying slabs and fags. They're just being lads, but there's more of an edge, a swagger, to their behaviour than the other kids who were mucking around under the lights before.

Neil keeps looking at her. 'Well, that's not good.'

She walks past the dogs. They bark at her and she shrinks a little. One of the young tradies comes out of the store and shushes the dogs. The girl doesn't look at him. But the man, maybe in his early twenties, looks at her.

The girl stares ahead and keeps on walking.

David says to Neil, 'We should give her a lift, maybe? I mean, it's your car, but . . .'

'Yeah, we should.'

They get into the old Land Rover and slowly drive past the store and the tradie, who is still looking after the girl. They pull up alongside the girl and she shrinks a little, turning away from them.

'Excuse me,' says David. The girl turns to look at him. She would be lucky to be fifteen, he thinks now. 'Are you right?'

She nods a little hesitantly.

'Look, do you need a lift?'

The girl stands, thinking.

'It's just that it's night-time and if you're thinking of trying to get a ride . . . Well, you probably shouldn't be hitchhiking.'

'I know.'

'Where do you want to go?'

'Nowhere. It doesn't matter. You're right. I shouldn't be hitching.'

David asks again, 'Where are you going?'

'Nowhere.'

'Nowhere?'

'Somewhere. I'm going somewhere, of course I'm going somewhere.' It's almost as if she is talking to herself.

'What's your name?'

'Evangeline. Evangeline de Rosso. Evangeline Beatrice de Rosso.'

David tries to suppress a smile. Neil grunts.

'We'll give you a lift,' David says.

'No thanks.' She thinks a bit and clicks her fingers together gently. She's holding a small mobile phone in her other hand. 'You are right, I shouldn't be hitching.'

'Well, can't you catch a bus?' asks Neil.

'The bus?'

'Have you got any money for the bus? There's a late run up to the top.'

'I've just spent a day on a bus.' She says 'bus' as if it was the vilest form of transport imaginable.

'You've got a phone there, haven't you?' David looks at the mobile in the girl's hand.

'Yes.' The girl answers as if she's talking to a three-year-old.

'So why not call someone?'

There is a pause until she realises that an answer is required before Neil will put the car in gear. 'No credit. Ran out.'

'Do you want to use one of our phones?'

The girl shrugs her shoulders. Maybe it's not belligerent or rude; perhaps she's just very shy, thinks David.

'We're heading up the escarpment, to the top. Is that any good for you?' he asks.

The other tradies barrel out of the general store full of energy for the rest of their night. The girl looks quickly in their direction and then back to David and Neil. 'So where are you going?' she asks.

'Up the escarpment,' says Neil. He looks at her some more. 'Too many questions? Sorry.'

'I don't see why everyone has to know everything.'

'Fair enough. We've all got secrets. We'll give you a lift if you like.'

She nods and then goes to the back passenger door, looks inside to see if it's okay and gets in. It's clear she feels awkward, as do David and Neil. David looks at his friend, who has a watchful magpie look in his eye.

As they drive past the beach, there are clouds piled high in greys and blues. The sea is greenish-grey in the bright moonlight and the sand yellow-pink.

Suddenly, the girl speaks. 'Beaches have the same colours as cities. Well, cities have the same colours as beaches. It's funny, isn't it? It's all blue and sand colours. Grey. Some nice greys.'

David turns around to her, impressed. 'What a great thing to notice. Are you – do you like art?'

'Yeah, it's all right. I like colours.'

'Pardon? Sorry.' David points to his ear then, surprised at what he has just done, turns away.

He can feel the girl looking at him as if to remind him that she thinks all old people are an annoying burden. 'Yeah,' she says.

He doesn't hear. Neil gives her a flick of his eyes and then looks ahead.

'Are you at art school?' says David, turning again.

The girl shrugs the question away.

David looks out at the view. 'I love colours, too,' he says, almost to himself.

The girl replies, but David only hears that she has spoken, not what she has said. He doesn't want to ask her to repeat herself again, so he just nods, pretending he has heard. The girl stares at him flatly. He has no idea what he has just agreed to. He turns back to look at the road, breathes a deep breath.

The road has started to snake its way up the escarpment in a series of S-bends and hills, the rainforest on either side forming a canopy, the lower layer lit by the Land Rover's headlights. David has his binoculars on his knees, hoping to see an owl.

A sign: *Cassowaries next 10 km*.

David turns to Neil. 'Seen any lately?'

'Not to speak of. Not unless I'm looking. Maybe only once in the last six months at the roadside. And one on the Cow Bay road. Some bastard had hit it.'

The girl speaks, reminding both of them they have a passenger. 'Did it die?'

Neil pauses, changing down a gear, then turns a little to reply to her while keeping his eyes on the road. 'One of the prettiest pieces of roadkill you can come across.'

'That's sad. How big was it?'

'Fully grown.'

'Yeah, but was it a female or a male?'

'It was a male.'

'That's sad; hope it didn't have chicks to look after. That would be really sad.'

'You got that right, sweetheart,' says Neil.

'They're all sad – the parrots, the doves, the birds of prey – when they're killed,' agrees David.

'I thought parrots and birds like that could always get out of the way,' says the girl.

'They might look like they can. They probably think it themselves, but the proof's lying by the roadside a bit too often.'

'What about animals, do animals get hit too?' asks the girl.

'Of course; sorry, both of us are bird men,' David explains. 'But yes, wallabies, possums, snakes. Sometimes feral cats and foxes – and that's on a good day. Even a feral dog – now that is a very good day. Bloody pests.'

As they come out of the rainforest and see the rolling hills lit by the moon, it's hard to believe they are in the same place. Paddocks with horses, small farms, patches of bush – but different from the rainforest – eucalypts and ferns and even some pines steepling up into the night.

A grunt from Neil and David looks ahead then quickly raises his binoculars. Before them he sees a large bird. It's a masked owl, perched on a road sign warning of a steep curve.

'On the road,' says Neil.

David shifts the bins and focuses. A bird of prey is pecking at some roadkill.

'Oh, it's a harrier! An Australasian harrier!' cries David. 'Lovely.'

'Good spot. Let's see what he's chomping down on.' Neil pulls up on the verge as the large bird, taking a hasty grab at the dead creature, flaps off, though only to the nearest tree, where David inspects it further through his binoculars.

The masked owl stares from the road sign.

Neil puts on his hazard lights and gets out, and David lowers his bins and opens his door.

'What are you doing?' The girl's voice is soft, betraying nervousness.

Neil doesn't hear her, moving to cross the road. David, barely picking up the words, opens her door. She *is* nervous. Not knowing why, he gestures for her to get out, too. She doesn't move.

Realisation comes to David. She is frightened, frightened of him – maybe of both of them. He is embarrassed, then feels a familiar anger. Why do those few dangerous men, or those thousands of dangerous men, leave good men to feel like this? Well, men who are just men.

David smiles, hoping to reassure her. 'We've just got to move whatever it is off the road. Otherwise any other birds that come along are likely to be hit, too. If we move it then the birds can feed safely.'

The girl nods, not moving. David holds his binoculars out for her. 'Want to have a better look at the owl – it's the one on the road sign – while I help Neil?'

She nods again, gets out and takes the binoculars. Leaning on the car, she points them at the owl. David goes over to Neil, who has picked up the flat creature, now recognisably a feral cat. He walks across the road and tosses it as far as he can, then turns and glances at David, who is scraping the animal's remains from the bitumen with the side of his shoe.

'A cat,' says Neil. 'A good day.'

David smiles, the girl smiles. They get back in the car.

They drive along in silence for a while. The tropical night has set in, still and warm. The headlights pick up the sugarcane lining the road.

A bird flies in front of them. Neil slows down, then he and David speak, almost in unison. 'Spur-winged plover!'

When the bird is safely past, Neil presses down on the accelerator. 'Bit late getting herself home,' he adds.

David doesn't reply, looking out the window.

Neil glances across at him then stares ahead, flicking his lights off full-beam as a car approaches, then back up again as it passes them.

'Where would you like us to take you?' Neil asks the girl.

'There's a turnoff. I'll know it when I see it,' she says. 'How many roads go up?'

'One.'

'Then it must be the right road,' she says.

'Yeah, I reckon you'd be right.'

'Do you mind if we just stop here at the lookout?' Neil asks her.

'No,' she says. 'You might see some birds.'

He pulls over and they stop to look at the view. David sees a tawny frogmouth camped in a low branch of a large tree, just to the side of the lookout. He ticks it off his list when he gets back in the car.

'Just a bit further, I think,' the girl tells Neil. 'If you

have to turn off, just drop me. This is the right road.'
A short pause, then, 'This is it.'

'Here?'

'Yes.'

'Cirillos'?' says Neil, surprised.

'Yes.'

'So I reckon you'd be Jas – young Jasmine?'

'Then I reckon you might be right.'

CHAPTER TWELVE

Clare can't quite believe she has sat on the chair reading to
Picnic the curlew for so long. As an audience, Picnic has
been pretty good, tilting her head this way and that and
only occasionally needing a bit of biscuit. And Clare couldn't
believe that she had read from, of all books, *Goldfinger*.
Not all of it, she reminded herself, only the bits that her
father had marked. And she couldn't quite believe how
entertainingly awful it was. She laughed frequently as she
read to the bird, and felt as though her father was somehow
a little closer to her.

She started reading at the scene where James Bond meets
Pussy Galore, who – astoundingly, given her name – is a

lesbian. The reader knows she's a lesbian because Bond feels a stirring in his loins that apparently all red-blooded males feel when they see a beautiful lesbian. Clare couldn't quite believe it was so, but this was what she read. To a bird who stood stock still and stared at her with deep brown, passive eyes.

Clare had put *Goldfinger* down, given another piece of biscuit to the bird and looked back into the chest for whatever else there was to read.

Underneath a pile of local papers, all open at the classifieds, was a large scrapbook. *Picnic Reads* was written very clearly on the cover in a neat draughtsman's hand. Inside, her father had marked a photocopy of a Philip Larkin poem. He'd also included pages from a copy of *A History of Australian Parrots*. He must have gone through his books and picked out his favourite bits of writing to read aloud.

Clare laughed at the eclectic contents. Dad, she thought, what fun you were. She never would have imagined her father was capable of such a vein of peculiar, lovely humour. He'd been an engineer, leaving behind his parents' farm for a career building roads and dams all around Australia. A man who had made a life of angles and percentages and equations and facts and certainty.

Now, Clare looks at the flying foxes moving overhead, the last birds settling, and listens to the sounds of the night animals. A few toads hop towards the lights on the verandah, staring angrily out at the land they are conquering. Then a car's lights shine down from the escarpment road and flash a hazy glow onto the lawn. She hears the car pull into the drive. She listens, hoping it will turn around and go away.

It isn't the birders; the last of the birding group had already settled into the lodges. They had arrived in two vans and got ready for the night ahead without much fuss. They all seemed quite old to Clare. One of the group, Don Barrellon, the one with a big beard and bits of twigs and branches everywhere – came over to thank her for opening the lodges to them.

'It's not a problem,' she told him. 'I'm happy to help. I just hope you'll all be comfortable.' She thought at the time that she wasn't too bad at being a host, after all.

'It's always comfortable here at Cirillos',' Don boomed, before his face softened. He looked at her and very gently took her hand. 'I know it's an imposition, and I know I'm a bit loud, but we're all so sorry about your father.'

All of a sudden, it became very hard for Clare not to cry. 'I'm sure Dad would have loved you being here,' she managed. 'Bit of a squeeze, but it's really an honour.'

And Don kept hold of her hand. That was awkward.

He looked like he was going to say something but thought better of it. Instead, he took a deep breath and let out an exhalation that smelled of tobacco. 'Oh,' he said. 'I'd better give that back to you.' And he released her hand.

Clare can see the headlights through the trees; the car has stopped. Then a figure emerges, silhouetted against the beams of light as he crosses in front of the vehicle and walks towards the gate. She turns off the verandah lights.

The interior car light comes on. She can see the vague outline of a person in the driver's seat.

She sits down again, feeling a rising sense of tension, of wanting to flee. Instinctively, she moves deeper into the shadows, making herself smaller, trying to disappear into the darkness.

The chain clinks as the gate is opened, and the car drives slowly towards the house.

Why she should feel so incapable of saying hello to whoever it is who has come to see her, or giving a slight wave or even offering a few words of welcome, a few meaningless pleasantries, she cannot fathom, yet it's her automatic reaction.

They're just people, she tells herself. She can hear Ollie's voice in her ears, his scorn at her idea of staying on here at the house, running a B & B.

She sees that Picnic, too, has remained motionless as the car approaches. She considers hiding then remembers the door is still open, so races back as inconspicuously as she can to close it so she isn't seen inside. Before she manages to do so, the bird turns its head slowly and stares up at her with those knowing eyes.

'No bickies now, Picnic,' Clare whispers. She ducks down below the windowsill just as the car's headlights sweep across the house, and the car stops.

Clare tries not to breathe, wills herself not to sneeze or cough.

Car doors open, footsteps sound on gravel.

Vague voices, female and male. Is it Neil? Christ, what does he want? Nothing, you stupid woman, she berates herself. He's probably brought you a cake, or a dead bird, or a friend of Picnic's . . . I don't know, just get up and open the door! You're an adult. He was nice. She reminds herself that it might not be him. It might be some more birders.

There is a knock on the door.

Clare hesitates, rises a little then remembers the wine glass in her hand and takes a little sip. She is momentarily impressed with herself. I certainly have my priorities right, bringing the wine and not spilling a drop, she thinks.

'I'm pretty sure I saw someone,' says a voice.

Clare swears silently.

'Are you sure?' It's Neil.

'Yeah, on the verandah,' says the other voice. 'Moved into the house, I thought.'

There is a silence. The flying foxes fill it with a bit of bickering over the fruit in the mango tree by the top corner of the garden.

'Is she your mum?' the second voice asks.

'Why do you say that?' asks Neil.

'Well, she just moved like – her, like Jasmine. The jizz was the same.'

Clare hears the voices. She almost stops breathing.

'Well, I'm going to go over to the lodge so maybe you can come there, too?' continues the same voice.

'I just accepted a lift. You're not responsible for me.' It's a girl's voice.

Clare breathes out then leaps up.

Whatever anybody was about to say is interrupted by the sudden illumination of the verandah as the front door opens and Clare stands there. The light is very bright. Picnic lets out a cry. Even David jumps.

'Stone curlew,' says David and he thinks of the myth.

'That'd be Picnic,' says Neil.

The bird cries again.

The Picnic Myth, thinks David randomly. That sounds like a good myth.

From the doorway, Clare takes in the picture before her: a man standing back beside the car, Neil beside the step, the girl raising her arm to knock again. Clare stares at her, her expression a mixture of surprise, fury and panic.

'So I guess she *is* your mother,' says David.

Clare looks down from the verandah to the man who has just spoken.

David looks up at the woman who has appeared at the door. It seems to him in that moment that he has just seen more emotions than an opera play across her face.

'Does your father know you're here?' Clare asks.

Jas shrugs.

Clare looks at David again, who stares back as her face closes down into impassivity and she glances at Neil. There is a pause.

Neil tries to fill it. 'We . . . um, met Jasmine downhill, just gave her a lift up. After she got off the bus.'

Clare nods her thanks.

'This is David Thomas, from Melbourne. He's a birder.'

Clare half-smiles.

'Thought it might be all right if he has a night or two at the lodge?'

Clare nods, Picnic calls again, and then a voice booms. Don Barrellon has made his way around from the lodge. 'David Thomas of Melbourne! Thought you might make it up the mountain.'

Clare looks at the enormous figure. David sees her hand tightening around the glass, her other hand anxiously clenching. He feels the tension.

'Hello, Clare.'

'Hello. Hello, Don.' Clare is suddenly very aware of the glass of wine in her hand.

'Well, you're starting the evening off in the appropriate vein, I see. Very good.'

'I'd offer you a glass but I was flat out managing to find this one.'

'Oh no, not a worry – we've come prepared with our own medications.' Don stops at the side of the steps, not far from Neil.

'Any luck?' asks David.

'No,' says Don. 'None at all. You?'

'Thought I might've seen it in silhouette, but there's no way I could be sure.'

'You'd have known if you'd seen it, David,' says Don.

Clare looks at Neil's friend and a veil falls across his face for a few moments before it is replaced with quite a nice smile.

'Well, that makes both of us, Don,' says David.

David Thomas of Melbourne. Clare bites her lip slightly. Why did she think that?

Don booms on, 'You after a bunk?'

David nods.

'Might be in trouble. We're full to the brim. Bit too cosy. We've got a shower, though, so you'll be a clean hobo for the night.'

David privately thanks God that Don has such a loud voice. He's heard everything Don's said. 'Well, look, I'm sure I'll squeeze in somewhere – I don't want to be a hassle.'

Clare looks at Jas, who stares blankly back at her mother. 'Why didn't you call?'

'My phone's out of credit. Ask them.'

David doesn't catch what the daughter has said but sees the anger in her mother's face. He turns to Neil, about to ask if he can maybe stay at his place after all, but remembers things are a bit 'iffy'.

'That's right, Clare. She said her phone was out of credit,' says Neil. 'I'd have David to stay at my place but, you know . . .' He lets the words hang in the air. David feels embarrassed for the mother.

'They gave me a lift when they didn't have to,' says the daughter.

Clare turns to David. 'Of course you can stay. We'll find a place.' She looks down at her daughter again. 'You'd better get inside.' Then, turning to Neil, 'Thanks, Murph.'

'Yeah, thanks,' says Jas.

'It's okay,' says Don. 'We'll find somewhere for him to throw his swag.'

Jasmine goes inside, and Clare smiles at the three men. ''Night,' she says, before closing the door.

Neil nods. 'A pleasure.' He raises his eyebrows at David. 'Well, I'll be seeing you tomorrow, hopefully. See you,

Picnic.' Then he walks over to his car, gets in and starts the engine.

Don grabs David's swag as David picks up his small backpack. 'So you didn't see it either?' He nudges David with a conspiratorial elbow. 'You sure?'

David looks back at the closed door of the house. He nods a yes to Don Barrellon. He looks at the curlew, which stands still and watches him.

There's a roll of thunder in the distance and the warmth of the evening presses all around. As he walks off with Don, David thinks. He thinks of something along the lines of a myth, of how it's rather odd that he could hear every word that Clare said to him. He remembers the way she held her glass. And how she sipped from it. And he thinks about her eyes. 'Quite lovely.'

'Yes, not a bad night at all,' says Don.

David reddens. He hadn't realised he had said his last thought out loud.

CHAPTER THIRTEEN

Inside the house Clare stares at Jas.

Her daughter shrugs her shoulders. 'What?'

'What are you doing here?'

'Oh, hi, Mum. It's good to see you, too.'

'Why are you here?'

'I just wanted to come. I just wanted to be here.'

'Does your father know you're here?'

Jas stares at her mother.

'What are you doing accepting lifts from strangers?'

'You *know* them!'

'I know Murph, not the other guy.'

'He seems nice. His name is David.'

'Did you ask for a lift? Were you hitchhiking?'

'Are you hearing yourself, Mum?' says Jas, armed with an arsenal of family anecdotes.

Yes – what do I sound like? Clare thinks. My father, that's what. One holiday up here years ago, when she was not much older than Jas is now, Clare had decided that she didn't want to spend any more time in the humidity and the rain. Her father had asked what was wrong. Why didn't his daughter smile anymore? 'Come on, sad sack, where is my laughing girl?'

She had just stared ahead, ignoring him.

Her mother had said from the kitchen, 'She's bored. She's a bit too good for us all of a sudden.'

Clare's nonna was on the sofa knitting. 'Oh, a princess now?'

Ollie had looked across from the sofa where he was holding a ball of wool for Nonna. His grandmother had tapped him on the head with a knitting needle and he looked back to the ball.

'Well,' said Clare's father, 'what are you going to do about it? It's a long way to Brisbane.'

She turned and stared out the window. 'There's nothing to do here,' she said.

'There are birds and books and a creek,' her father said. 'What more do you want?'

She had shrugged her shoulders.

'Too good for us,' said Nonna.

Later, after lunch, Clare had walked out the back door and through the orchard to where the road led down to the general store at the bottom of the escarpment. She walked with her Gear-and-Stuff bag, a family Christmas present, in one hand, while in the other she held out a piece of cardboard that had been ripped from the top of a cardboard box. In bubble writing, each letter a different colour, was *BRISBANE*.

She had made it halfway to the general store when she had to take off her cork-soled sandals that had been another present. She put on the beach thongs, a stocking filler.

Once, a car had passed, then slowed. An angry-looking sort of car – a utility van with three people in the front cabin and a couple of dogs in its tray. Were they checking her out? She heard a laugh before it sped off. She was frightened, but decided to walk on anyway. They were laughing at her back there in the house, too. She walked three-quarters of the way down the escarpment when the new rubber thongs began to cut into the skin between her big toe and her second toe. And then it had started to rain. To pour. A thunderstorm.

She had stood with her Gear-and-Stuff bag over her head and her texta sign, the colours running. A car stopped. It frightened her anew, and she thought she might be about to cry when she heard his voice.

'Are you trying to hitchhike? To Brisbane on the thumb?'

She had stood there in the rain and looked at her father.

'Well, there you go,' he said.

They stared at each other for a good while until, eventually, she walked around and got into the seat next to him.

He had said nothing. Just smiled, turned the car around and drove back to the house.

'Did you hitchhike?' she says again now.

'Mum – I caught the bus. You heard what they said.' Jas's voice is filled with the kind of mocking disdain only a teenage daughter can convey. 'It's not like *you* never hitchhiked, is it?'

Jas was right. Although on that one occasion her father had picked her up and taken her home, Clare had hitchhiked many times, before and since. She wished she hadn't admitted as much to her daughter.

'I'm going to ring your father.'

'Fine. Do that.'

Clare went to the phone, feeling angry. Angry at being caught out, surprised she's no longer alone.

She dials the number. It takes a long time for the phone to engage – for each number she has to put a finger in the hole of the old-fashioned phone and wrench the dial around. Jas hides a laugh.

Clare looks at her while the phone rings at the other end. 'Don't laugh at me.'

Jas stops.

The phone is answered. She hears his voice. 'Hello?'

She listens.

'Hello?'

She used to hear it a lot, she thinks. It used to be a voice that was hers.

'Hello?'

'Hello, Gary, it's Clare.'

'Clare, how are you?' There is a slight change in the tone.

'Jas has just turned up.'

There's a pause. 'Well, that's good. Thanks for letting me know.'

She can hear the kids' voices in the background. And, she supposes, what must be *her* voice.

'You knew she was coming here?'

'Yes, she told me you wanted her to come up.'

'She did?' says Clare, watching a gecko make its way across the brick arch into the next room.

Jas stares back, watching her mother on the phone.

'Who is it, hon?' says a woman's voice.

Clare hears a muffled, 'It's Clare,' from the receiver.

There's a pause and then the woman's voice says, 'Oh, well – say hi. Hope she's well.'

Cow, thinks Clare. She means what she's saying, though; she is a very nice woman. Cow, Clare thinks, regardless.

'Yeah, look, Clare – we did have something planned for the holiday break but you wanted Jas with you so, you know . . . I don't know why you insisted she take the bus. I mean, if we just talked a bit more we could've sorted something out. We could have paid for the plane.' He stops speaking. The kids in the background squabble, then a little girl's voice calls for her father.

Clare stares up at the gecko on the arch. 'I *wanted* her?' she says slowly.

'Well, that's what she said. Is everything all right?' he sounds vaguely worried.

'No, everything is fine. I'm just letting you know that she's arrived safely.'

There's another pause.

'That's all,' says Clare.

'Good,' says Gary. 'Thanks for letting me know. You okay?'

'Yes,' says Clare, 'I'm okay.'

'All right then . . . Tamsin says hi.'

'Good, say hello back.'

'Right. Bye.'

'Bye.' He hangs up and another house full of a life that isn't hers disappears. The gecko crawls further up the wall and chirps, a sound like someone cleaning glass with a moist cloth, which is slightly irritating if you are in the mood to be irritated.

Clare stares at the lizard. She's in the mood.

Jas is standing, daring her to speak.

The gecko chirps.

How can she explain? How do you tell a girl, your daughter, what those voices down the end of the line mean? A nice man who used to be your husband, a kind man, who cared for you. A man who is your daughter's father. To Clare those voices mean her daughter's home and her ex-husband's new life with a nice woman, who isn't grumpy or shy or awkward. Who didn't get sick and who knows when to shut up, who knows when fairness doesn't matter.

Maybe that's not fair, Clare thinks. The gecko chirps. She's just a person. I wanted choices. No one's to blame for what happened to me.

The gecko again.

She stares at the lizard, takes a sip of wine. She looks at her daughter. Jas looks older. She always does these days, whenever Clare sees her. They'll hug, she supposes, to say hello.

Not like in times past, when Jasmine would grab Clare with all her might, hold on to her. Clare remembers one particular occasion, the afternoon of Jas's first day at school. Clare had stood outside the gates and waited. Jas had waved a little as her new teacher led her out of the classroom. Her new best-friend grown-up, Clare supposed. The grown-up she would – every day for a year – get to know; then, at the end of that year, the teacher would stay behind to greet new children, and another teacher would take her place in Jas's life.

The beginning of a lifetime of saying goodbye.

Clare gave a small wave back. The little girl shifted her shoulders slightly and played with a strap on her new school backpack as she walked up to her mother. Clare knelt down and the little girl, her daughter, hugged her, held her as if she would never see her mother again. Clare thought that she would never let go. And her little daughter clung to her for what seemed like an hour, hugging her as if it was not a welcome but a goodbye; there was sorrow there somewhere.

The gecko chirps. It does sound like a glass being cleaned.

It was just a hug. The kind of hug she doesn't get anymore. A hug from when Jas liked being with her, wanted to learn everything Clare knew. A time when hugs were common and easy, unimpeded by Jas's new hated breasts, her self-conscious prickliness. Well, Clare only supposes that is how her daughter feels; she had felt that way when she was that age, when changes started happening to her body, to her world.

What had really changed was trust. Jas had trusted her absolutely, thought that the way Clare did things was the good way, the definitive way. How had she lost the trust? Why? Was it just normal, just part of growing up? Jas forming her own opinions, tearing loose from their twosome? Or had she been torn? Clare suddenly pictures them on the morning walk to primary school, Jas tucked alongside her the whole way, her arm reaching up around her mother's waist, teasing her about the bit of fat on her sides. Calling one side Peter Chubs, the other Paul Chubs. Her own tummy was called George.

'George is hungry,' Jas used to say, sweet-voiced. 'George thinks an icy pole at recess is good for concentration.'

A clever funny girl; *her* clever funny girl.

'So I wanted you to come, did I?' Clare says.

'Did you?' says Jas.

'Of course I did. How's George?'

Jas looks back blankly then smiles as she remembers. 'He's hungry.'

'Well, we can't have that.'

Jas then mimics Clare furiously dialling the number on the old phone. It's funny and Clare's face splits into a laugh.

And then Jas hugs her. Hugs Clare.

The gecko chirps. It sounds quite sweet.

David walks into one of the lodges and is met with what feels like a very familiar sight. These are 'his' people, he supposes, a group of rather elderly folk dressed in browns and dark blues.

Well, he thinks, there's old and there's old, but in all honesty I would be one of the youngest here.

There are about a dozen of them, neatly setting out their gear near their allotted bunk. The three pickers' cabins are all full.

Even though David knows a few of these birders, they all look at him with a wary kind of friendliness. They accept him as one of their own but ruffle with a protectiveness of their territory. Right now, supposes David, these people just want to be certain of a bed for the night, and they regard him not so much a fellow traveller as a bit of a burden, half-pitying looks crossing their faces, like passengers in a full lifeboat when they see another survivor paddling towards them.

Helen waves to him. 'You'll have a time of it finding a bed here, I'm afraid,' she says loudly.

As lifeboat knockbacks go, it is better than being beaten off back into the dark waters with a shove in the face from an oar. 'Well now, I'm just after a shower,' says David. 'Then I'll work out where I'm going to park myself for the night.'

A man David doesn't recognise clutches his tartan toiletries bag and a couple of toothbrushes. 'There's a bit of a queue. A bit of a queue for the shower; there used to be two, used to be. Now there's just the one, just the one. The one shower.'

David nods. He doesn't know if the man is repeating himself for David's benefit. He hears Don's bird call in his ear.

''Fraid you'll have to wait a bit, David Thomas of Melbourne. In fact, you'd have to be at the bottom of the list.'

'Well, there used to be the other shower, the other one, but it's not working. Yes, not working,' says the man with the tartan toiletries bag. He waves two toothbrushes like a conductor of an orchestra might wave a baton.

'That's about the size of it, David Thomas.'

'Not working,' repeats the man.

'This is David Thomas from Melbourne,' says Don.

'Clive. Clive Farquhar. Clive Farquhar from Adelaide,' says the toothbrush-holder.

'Hello, Clive,' says David.

'Hello. It's Clive. Farquhar,' says Clive, holding his tartan bag.

'From Adelaide,' says David, smiling.

'Yes, from Adelaide,' says Clive. 'Clive Farquhar.'

They all stand there, David smiling, Don smiling, Helen smiling, Clive clutching his tartan toiletries bag. And waving his toothbrushes.

'I'm a dentist. A dentist,' says Clive Farquhar of Adelaide. 'Retired. But I still like to keep my hand in. That's why I've got two brushes – one for my teeth, one for my tongue.'

'Right,' says David.

'Thought you might have thought it a bit odd. Bit odd, the two brushes.'

'A tongue brush?' says Helen loudly.

'Yes, yes, a tongue brush,' says Clive, even louder.

'Why a tongue brush?' asks Helen.

'Why a tongue brush? Well now, well now, a tongue brush. It's actually – its proper name is a tongue *cleaner*.'

'That so?' says Don.

'Tongue cleaner. And the tongue is fascinating.'

David nods. He can't think of anything to say.

'Fascinating. What do you think the tongue is?' continues Clive. 'Helen?'

'Pardon? The tongue – what?'

'What do you think it is?'

'The tongue?'

'Yes.'

'What do you mean?'

'What do I mean?'

Holy Christ, thinks David.

'Yes.'

'Well, what *is* it? Is it a muscle?'

'Is the tongue a muscle?' ponders Helen.

'Yes, is it a muscle?' repeats Clive, even louder.

'No, Clive – I heard you.'

'Oh,' says Clive.

'Is it a muscle . . .' repeats Helen.

Clive waves his tongue brush.

'Well,' says Don Barrellon, 'it would have to be.' And he gives a bird call.

'Yes, it would probably be a muscle,' agrees Helen.

'A muscle, you think? Well, you're wrong. Wrong!' says Clive. 'Tissues make up an organ, and many organs make up a system. The tongue – your tongue, my tongue, all our tongues – is more than just tissue. The tongue's a part of the digestive system and I consider it to be an organ of the digestive system, even though many would say it's a muscle.'

'Yes,' says Helen.

'Yes,' confirms Clive Farquhar. 'And a tongue is in need of a cleaner. The tongue cleaner is very important as far as oral hygiene goes. Very important.'

'Well . . .' says Don Barrellon.

'Well, indeed, because there's a fair deal of bacterial build-up and food debris and dead cells on the surface of the tongue. And without cleaning, you can get a build-up, which will lead down the path of . . .'

Nobody says anything.

'Halitosis!' cries Clive, animatedly. 'The most common cause of bad breath is the build-up of decaying cells and bacteria upon the surface of your tongue.'

'Well, really,' says Helen.

'And that is why I have two brushes,' says Clive, waving them towards himself. 'Two brushes, and it's the cleaner that comes in very handy for some of us.'

Don gives a bird call.

David thinks that there might be a point about Clive needing the second brush. Or cleaner. Oh Christ, he thinks again.

Nadia, Helen's 'ears' from the beach that morning, enters the room, fresh from the shower. 'I bet you're a Virgo, Clive. You sounded very Virgoan from the shower; very particular.'

'Well, no, not a Virgo, just a retired dentist – who happens to be in need of the shower.'

He moves off and Nadia calls after him, 'What star sign are you then, Clive?'

He turns back at the door and gives a salute with his brushes. 'Taurus. A Taurean dentist.' He leaves the room.

'A Taurean dentist,' repeats Nadia.

The Taurean dentist. David nods, then thinks of the night he spent in the reclined seat of the Tarago. And the sleep he didn't get. And the fact that he has gone two days without a shower. Two days of travel and of birding and of being bogged and covered in mud and getting sandfly bites on the back of his neck.

'I really need a shower,' he says.

'Well now, David Thomas,' says Don, 'Clare told us yesterday that we can use the outdoor shower at the back of the shed if we want. No hot water, though.'

'Yes,' says Nadia. 'No hot water, and the tank water is freezing at this time of year.'

She looks as if she might be about to start on star signs again, so David decides a shower is a shower. 'I think I'll give it a try.'

He grabs his gear and walks back up towards the house. Crossing the grass, he takes a couple of cautious second glances at some cane toads. One especially large one rotates slightly in his direction as he passes.

He goes up the steps to the front door and is about to knock when he hears a noise from inside. He can't quite work out what it is, whether it is laughter or crying. He stands with his hand to the door, not knowing what to do.

It is Jas who breaks the hug. Quite abruptly. At first Clare thinks she must have rememberd she is sixteen and that teenagers aren't meant to hug their parents. Especially the parent they don't like, the 'problem' parent. But it was a nice hug.

Clare looks at her.

Jas cocks her head towards the door. 'What was that? Mum, did you hear that?'

Clare listens. There is the sound of a footstep, then another, walking down the stairs. Then, before Clare can think what to do, they change direction and step closer to the door.

'Who's there?' she cries, making Jas jump. 'Hello? Who's there?'

Then there's a knock; it's very loud.

Both mother and daughter jump.

David hadn't meant to knock so loudly but the cry of 'Who's there?' had startled him, making him bring his fist down a lot harder than he had intended.

Clare stands behind the closed door with Jas behind her. 'Yes?' she asks through the wood.

'Oh, I'm sorry,' David replies. 'I got a bit of a fright when you yelled.'

'I yelled?' says Clare, in a tone that makes both Jas and David on the other side of the door slightly alarmed.

'Oh, Mum,' whispers Jas.

'Sorry. I didn't mean you yelled. Well, not in any bad way. Well, I suppose it was a bit of a yell . . .'

Clare opens the door. And there stands the man. The man who had looked at her. Murph's friend. The one covered in mud. And he is doing it again; David stands looking at Clare. Then his eyes move to the wine glass she holds in her hand.

Clare follows his gaze. 'It's the same one,' she says.

'Pardon?' says David.

'It's still the same wine.'

'Oh, Mum,' whispers Jas again. And she giggles.

'Are you okay? Can I help you?' Clare asks him.

And David looks at her, really looks at her. He might even have been staring. And his one hope, of all things, is that his tongue is clean.

And so he smiles.

CHAPTER FOURTEEN

It is a nice enough smile, thinks Clare, but then he starts doing something odd with his tongue, as if he is trying to scrape it against his top teeth. He looks at her and stops.

David silently curses Clive Farquhar of Adelaide. He thinks of perhaps trying to explain. Trying to explain – what? What he just did with his tongue? Why he'd listened to a retired dentist who was on some tongue-cleaning crusade? Could he blame a piece of shower-queue chitchat for his tongue indiscretion? No, he thinks, I should just ask for a shower, be polite and leave it at that.

'Can I help you?' asks Clare.

'Yes, sorry to interrupt. I hope . . . Well, sorry. I'm . . . I just really need a shower.' He gestures to his muddy legs. 'I'm sorry,' he repeats, 'I know I said I wouldn't be a hassle but there is quite a queue of needy birders for the shower in the lodge and I'm way down on the list.' Don't do that thing with your tongue, he tells himself.

Clare nods.

'And I'd just like to get the mud off and wash my sandfly bites . . .' He pats the back of his neck. 'And, you know . . .'

She stares at him.

'So Don told me about the shower out the back?'

A shadow falls across Clare's face and she thinks she should never have told the hairy man about the shower. That was when she was trying to be a host. 'Yes.' She sounds annoyed, she realises, and gets even more annoyed by her annoyance.

David takes a breath and steps back. 'Um, I'm sorry; could I use the shower? The outside one?'

'Yes,' says Clare.

'Could you show me where it is, please?'

'Oh,' says Clare.

'Or just tell me?'

Yes, the shower, thinks Clare. 'Yes, of course.'

David nods. 'Thanks.'

She stands at the door; well, he can't come through the

house, he's too muddy. I'll take him around the verandah, she thinks.

David bends to pick up his swag and backpack just as Clare steps forward, walking into his head. They both jump back.

'Sorry,' says Clare.

'Sorry,' says David.

There's a sound from inside the house. Clare looks behind her to see Jas laughing.

Then mother and daughter give each other a fierce glare. David thinks that maybe star signs and waiting in line for the shower wasn't such a bad option after all. He's obviously interrupted something. He runs his tongue over his teeth again, groans and swallows a curse.

Clare turns away from her daughter to look at him. He stops scraping his tongue.

'Let's go this way around the verandah,' she says, pointing.

David nods, standing back so Clare can step outside. 'Look, thank you for this. I know it's a bit awkward.'

'No, it's fine.'

'Well —'

'It's okay.' She is back to trying to be a host.

David can't help himself. 'That thing I just did with my tongue . . .' He can't believe he has just said this.

Neither can Clare. 'Pardon?' she says.

Jas snorts a laugh, and Clare closes the door on her.

'Look, sorry,' says David. 'I'm really sorry for interrupting you and I know that things – well, that they aren't great. But that – that tongue thing . . .' He is embarrassed.

Jas opens the door again.

'That tongue thing,' he repeats, knowing he has to keep going now. 'You know . . .' He scrapes his tongue against his teeth. Clare stares. 'It's awful. Result of a conversation with a dentist – a retired dentist from Adelaide, who was waiting for a shower in the lodge. All about good breath. I've never done it before. Like a bowerbird displaying – after he's thrown his bits of colour in front of the bower, he dances, flicking his tongue all over the place.' David stops; perhaps these two aren't birders. 'When he's after a —'

'When he's trying to impress a female,' says Jas.

Clare looks to her daughter then back to David. 'Oh, you're trying to impress me with your tongue?' she asks.

So like her daughter, thinks David, grimacing.

'The shower's this way.'

They head off – David, Clare and Jas. Clare is poised to say something to Jas but then changes her mind. David thinks she'll say something later.

'You know a bit about birds, then?' says David.

Clare is about to respond when she realises that the question was meant for Jas.

'A bit. I've just started. Pop was a mad birder.'

'Your grandfather was a *great* birder,' says David. 'And a gentleman. He was a gentle man and a gentleman.'

'Did you know him?' asks Jas. Clare wishes she would shut up.

'Only a bit, but we did see a cracking bird once.'

'Which one?' Jas says.

'Well, it was a Gouldian finch.'

Clare looks at him. 'You saw a Gouldian finch with my father?'

David nods. 'In Katherine.'

'In the wild?' asks Jas.

'Yes. We were spotting together. It was a birding tour and we'd only just met. But we got lucky, and about halfway through the twitch we saw the Gouldian. In the wild.'

'How did you feel?'

'It was a hoot. Your pop, he was a good man to spend a day with. He knew the value of good conversation.'

Clare wishes he would shut up. Jas keeps asking him questions, which irritates her even more.

'Did you come up to see the bird? The PPMG?'

David smiles. 'Yes. All the way from Melbourne. Doesn't look like I'll get lucky this time; I have to get back tomorrow. Neil reckons the bird has pushed off.'

'Mum lives in Melbourne,' says Jas.

Clare stops and points to the shower at the back of the shed. It's connected to a large water tank that stands on a platform beside it. 'Well, there you go. There's a light.' She switches it on. 'I'm afraid it's not heated.'

David holds up a hand. 'Please – it's fine, and thank you again.'

Clare nods.

'Will you look for the bird tomorrow?' Jas asks.

'Yes, but I don't know how we'll go if this rain comes.'

'Can I come with you? Maybe I can bring you some of Pop's luck.'

'Jas!' Clare admonishes.

'Well, that's what I wanted to come up here for. To see the bird,' Jas says.

Clare gives her a look of disbelief.

'That and to see what you're going to throw away,' Jas says to her mother.

'What, don't you trust me?'

'Well, you might not know what's important, what Pop might have wanted to keep. Those piles are there for a reason.'

Clare wants to scream at Jas – if it's a fight she wants then she can have it. But just in time she remembers David. 'Look, I'm sorry, we'll leave you to the shower,' she says to him. 'Let's go, Jas.'

'But I'd like to go birding, to see the —'

'Jas . . .'

David doesn't say anything. The three stand there. Then Jas turns abruptly and Clare follows. David fumbles in his backpack for his toiletry bag and towel.

Mother and daughter are on their way back to the verandah when they hear him groan. They both turn around.

'I've left – I've left my towel and wash stuff in the bloody cream-bun sub!'

Clare and Jas look at him, uncomprehending.

'My rental car. It's down at the service station. Locked.'

The two women stare at him.

'Would it be all right if you take me? Birding?' Jas asks.

Clare is really angry.

David just wants to have a shower. 'Look, Jas —'

Clare cuts him off. 'I saw a black-throated finch today. It was dead.' She can't help herself, being competitive.

Jas looks at her. Clare nods back at Jas. And at David.

'Oh,' he says.

Clare feels slightly silly and says, 'Yes.'

'Pretty bird,' says David.

'Pretty *dead* bird,' says Jas and she walks off.

'Would you like to borrow a towel and some . . .' Clare pauses. 'Some washing stuff?'

'Would you mind? I'm very sorry.' Star signs would have been a *much* better bet.

'Right,' says Clare. She stops and then adds, 'Do you remember much about my father?'

'Well, I only spent a day with him, but . . .' He trails off, thinking.

Clare waits.

'He taught me quite a lot. About how something you may think is a hassle isn't really. It's a gift that the world gives you to make you think a little.' He laughs. 'Taught me all about time gifts.'

Clare looks at David. He is a bit odd; well, he is a birder. A bit odd, but . . . She doesn't let herself go there. Instead she nods and says, 'You're right about the tongue thing. It's a bit strange.' Then she moves away, in search of soap and a towel.

David watches her go. He's not sure, but he thinks she left with a hint of a smile on her face. Ah, I like that, he decides. And he cleans his tongue.

Jas is waiting for Clare inside the house.

'What do you think you're doing, asking if you can go birding with him?' Clare demands.

'I want to go.'

'You don't know a thing about him! First you get into

a car with him and now you want to go wander around the bush with him!'

'He knew Pop!'

'*We* don't know anything about him. Don't be so stupid!'

'You're stupid. You! "I saw a dead black-throated finch." Stupid.'

Clare tries hard not to shout. 'Why are you here? And don't just stand there and shrug your shoulders.'

'I wanted to see the bird. The pale pygmy magpie goose. Pop saw it once; he told me it was a special bird. And I don't want you throwing his stuff away. You can't – it's his.' The girl's voice rises in anger. 'You can't just throw everything away like you always do. I hate you!'

Clare looks at her daughter, caught in that land between childhood and a looming life as an adult. Jas is all grown up in some ways, in others still a baby, a product of helicopter parenting. Never getting out of the shower in the morning until someone has banged on the door for a fifth time; never listening to anybody she's related to who is over the age of thirty. And she's the product of a family that fell apart; of a mother who got sick, a father who returned when Clare was ill and left again when she didn't want him to stay anymore.

How do you explain to a young girl that her father is a man you fell out of love with? A man who isn't the 'one' after all? He's just another nice man now, with a new family and a younger, prettier, nicer second wife. With new children and an extra bedroom for the child from his first, failed marriage.

How do you explain to a girl that her mother can make a mistake, or that she just got bored or wanted to make a choice or got sick with cancer?

Clare suddenly feels as if she's about to cry, not for herself but for her daughter. For Jas, the little girl who held her hand in the hospital ward and stared at her with fear and uncertainty, wondering why her mum was lying there, looking so scared and tearful; for how, months later, she had seen her mother in the shower and looked at the long scar that travelled across her chest in place of the breast that had been excised by the smiling people, the smiling people who had visited the bed in the hospital ward as Jas held her mother's hand.

'This is Mr Fox, he's a surgeon,' Clare had whispered to her daughter.

Her pop, Clare's father, had stroked Jas's hair and said, 'Mr Fox is going to help your mum. He's going to make her better.'

And Mr Fox had turned to Jas with a polite smile that wasn't really his, had stood above her and said in a voice that was as clear as the bright lights in the hospital and just as distant, 'Well, I've tried my best, and we'll certainly look after your mummy.'

Jas had looked to her mummy, Clare, for confirmation that the smiling people could be trusted to fix things. So Clare had nodded.

Clare had never meant to show the scar to her daughter – she could barely look at it herself – and so when the little girl had walked into the bathroom when Clare was drying herself after the shower, it was almost as if she was looking at the scar for the first time, through the eyes of her daughter. She had stood there, frozen, while Jas stared at her chest.

The little girl who had held her hand and given her drawings of smiling flowers and suns and happy dogs while she was in hospital. Who had remained brave and strong through all her treatments. Through the tension, the nervousness of preparing for trips to the doctor, through the endless weeks of nausea and the wretchedness of the chemotherapy, knowing not to touch Clare or give her hugs because her mother just needed rest and a chance to get better.

That day in the bathroom, Clare had sat down on the rim of the bath and beckoned to her daughter. Jas had walked slowly towards her, looking first at the scar and then at her mother. The breast upon which she had suckled, with which Clare had nurtured and fed her.

'Will it grow back again?' said her little girl.

Clare had smiled and said quietly, 'No.'

'But they said . . . the hospital people said you'd get better.' Her lip had trembled and the tears had fallen.

Clare had reached for her daughter then, and had tried to hold her, and her little girl had cried, great gulping drowning sobs.

And then, when Jas was older, the way she stared at her mother and screamed – screamed with all her strength – that she hated her, that she hated Clare for telling her father to leave, for telling him that she didn't love him. She had pulled away from Clare's hug in protest.

It was almost primal, the girl's belief that she was being wronged, that her parents were being torn apart, and by someone she had trusted, her mother. Torn apart? Drifted was perhaps closer to the truth, drifted beyond any hope of returning. Drifted without any intention from Clare to do anything about it. Clare knew then, as she does now, that it was a choice she'd made. But try explaining that to her teenager.

Clare had tried to tell her daughter that sometimes people – grown-ups – fall out of love, and it's better, then, for them to be apart. 'I hate you,' she had said. 'I hate you.'

Again, Clare feels the blow. But Jas couldn't accept it. In her mind, it was as if Clare had thrown away Jasmine's father. She can almost understand Jasmine's anger but still she feels the blow.

'I hate you.'

'I was just trying, I'm just trying . . .' But she can't finish her sentence. 'I don't know why you came here if you hate me so much.'

Jas replies like a five-year-old on automatic, 'Well, it feels like you hate *me* sometimes.'

Clare swallows, tries not to respond in kind, but fails. 'When? What? What have I done to you? I love you, Jas. You've been wonderful about my —'

Jas interrupts. '*Been!* Not anymore.'

Clare is completely exasperated. 'I didn't mean that!'

Jas shrugs rudely. 'Whatever.'

Clare rounds on her daughter, gloves off. 'Maybe it is "been". I hardly see you. You chose to go and live with your father.'

'Well, you chose to not stay married!' Jas yells. 'If you'd been nicer to Dad he wouldn't have left. Dad was so good to you.'

Clare closes her eyes, her mouth tight in an effort not to make another knee-jerk reply. Unspoken, the words tumble around her brain, banging into each other, repeating and contradicting, thudding into her skull until it throbs.

Fuck. Fault. Truth. No truth. Whose truth? Fuck. He *had* been so good. But what's 'good'? Good to the prickly, picky, pitiful. A saint, full of pity. He'd left her for his new girlfriend and then come back like the cavalry when he had found out she was sick. 'I can't just leave,' he had said.

He probably had never stopped seeing that woman. And he had come back, come back and looked after her. He had moral superiority when it came to decision-making. So she had got in first. 'It's all over now, let's move on,' she had said. Bastard! New wife, a son and a baby daughter to get right this time. Bastard. Why did he get Jas, too? Because Jas had chosen to go with him.

Clare opens her eyes. Her daughter is still staring at her, a combination of fear and bravado showing on her face.

Clare's head is really throbbing now. She speaks relatively calmly. 'I might have been able to be nicer to him. But I could never be prettier, or younger or – new.'

She pauses, thinks about the other thing her daughter said. 'Some of this stuff, Pop's stuff, is just junk.'

'You don't know!'

'Some of it *is*!' Clare grabs a magazine that is lying on the sideboard. It's an old agricultural magazine on water-pumping, yellowed and rat-nibbled at the edges. 'This was probably on its way to the recycling bin.'

Jas stares.

'We can go through this stuff together, and you can stay for the holidays.'

'I want to try and see the bird. It was in a birding newsletter.'

'When did your pop talk to you about birding?' Clare's tone is accusatory and she wishes she had not said it.

'Last year. Mid-term break last September. I came up here for a week. He showed me his books.'

Clare remembers. Jas had come up to the orchard and then spent the next week of the holidays with her in Melbourne. When she had asked her daughter what she and her grandfather had done, Jas had just shrugged her shoulders and said, 'Usual stuff.'

'We used to email each other about birds – he told me the best time to see the PPMG was about now. You can check his computer if you want to, if you don't believe me.'

Clare had never thought to check the old Apple Mac that sat on the desk among all the clutter of her father's study. That had been his thing – a part of his bird and dam and engineering world, as alien to her as any parent's hobby or idiosyncratic interest may be. The computer was his thing, and maybe Jas's too.

'Just wait,' Clare tells Jasmine. Why she says that she has no idea, but it gives her a bit of time to think about how best to deal with the sudden appearance of her daughter.

She stomps off to the bathroom at the back of the house and gets some soap, shampoo and a towel, hesitates over powder and moisturiser, adds deodorant, then the moisturiser and insect repellent, and puts them all in a basket. On her way out she stops and goes back to the small cabinet under the sink and reaches for a gold tin. Back in the kitchen she asks Jas to take it out to David.

'Me? No way! First you hate me for getting a lift with him, and then you say I can't go birding because we don't know anything about him and now you want me to go out in the dark and give him soap!' Jas rummages through the basket. 'And some shampoo, and some spray of something, and this.' She holds up the tin of Rawleigh's. 'Maybe I could wash his back for him, too?'

Clare breathes out. 'I don't hate you. I don't not trust you and I don't not want you to be here. I was worried and surprised and these people – these bird people – are —'

'Are just going to be here for a day or two,' says Jas.

Realising she has no ground to stand on, Clare takes the basket out to David herself.

David is puffing a little and filling up his water bottle from the tap. 'I thought I'd better check the shower was all right; had a peek up there and the mesh filter net is fine. So I thought I might as well pinch a bit of water for tomorrow.'

Clare nods. 'Cold?'

'No, well, yes – beautiful, cleanest water in the world.'

'Okay.'

'Thanks again for this.'

'That's fine. I'll, um, be inside if you need anything. You can put your swag just around on the side verandah if you want. You'll be dry there if it rains and there's a mossie

net set up on the daybed so, you know, go for your life.'
Clare turns to leave.

'That sounds great, thank you.'

She remembers something else. 'There's some insect repellent in the basket, just in case, and a tin of Rawleigh's salve for your sandfly bite.'

'Rawleigh's? Sounds like a whisky or a packet of smokes!'

'It's just an old salve,' says Clare, 'for bites and stuff.'

'Well, thanks for that – really.'

'Do you need anything else?'

'I think I should be right. I might pop back down to the lodge and see if Don's gang are going to go through the day's birds. I should be right. Thanks again.'

Clare nods and walks back into the house.

This evening has moved too fast for her. She's said things she didn't want to say. She doesn't want her daughter to leave. Yet she liked being here on her own, feeling that perhaps she could stay here for a while.

CHAPTER FIFTEEN

Jas isn't in the kitchen when Clare returns. She looks in the living room. She's not there either.

'Jas?' she calls. No answer.

She repeats the call, louder this time. She hears her own voice, a little more worried than she intended.

She is about to call out again when Jas responds, flatly, 'In here.'

Following the sound, Clare goes into her father's study. Jas is sitting at the desk. She stops what she's doing and stares impassively at her mother. Clare looks away. Looking at Jas is like looking at a mirror image of herself in another time. She wants to hug or soothe her daughter, tell her how much she loves her. Typical Clare, she thinks, swinging from one end of the spectrum to the other. Instead she says, lamely, 'You're on the computer.'

She walks over to the desk and stands just behind Jas. There on the screen is a list of email messages from Jas. Clare reads over her shoulder. Some are simple one-line questions: *How do you tell the difference between a magpie and a currawong? What is the difference between a crow and a raven? Do northern crows talk differently from the southern ones? Are they a different type of crow?*

While Clare watches, Jas opens a longer message: a description of a birding trip to the Boondall Wetlands in Brisbane, stories of the birds she saw, the people she was with. Another message lists fifteen birds seen during two days of travelling to and from school. Then there is a question from Jas: *Ten birds I should try to see before I am twenty?*

Clare reads out her father's response: 'Darling Jasmine, here is your pop's golden list!' The old man had insisted there was no order required. 'Gouldian finch, orange-bellied parrot (in the wild), grey goshawk, light-mantled sooty albatross (see great wanderer, same conditions apply), pale pygmy magpie goose, great wandering albatross (at sea, off the continental shelf), scarlet-chested parrot, plains wanderer, princess parrot, southern cassowary.' There are names in the list that hold some meaning for Clare: the Gouldian finch, the grey goshawk. She laughs.

Jas looks up at her, and Clare explains, 'We used to call the grey goshawk the "Hot Diggity" because Dad, your pop, came back one night after traipsing around the forest all day singing this awful song, "Hot Diggity" by a guy called Perry Como.'

'The Hot Diggity bird,' says Jas. 'I heard him say that.'

Clare nods. 'The Hot Diggity bird,' she repeats, and laughs her big open laugh. 'He'd say that when he was happy, "Hot Diggity!" – or when he was excited about something. That or "Well, there you go."'

Jas laughs too. 'Well, there you go,' she says, mimicking her grandfather. She looks at her mother again. 'Have you gone through the stuff on this computer?'

'No, but your uncle Ollie said he checked it for a few things, just for the estate. I didn't really want to go through it – I mean, it's sort of personal.'

'I wouldn't want this stuff just to disappear, though,' says Jas softly. 'I mean he – Pop – might have other stuff on it for me, stuff that he was going to send.'

Clare is quiet.

'Look here, Mum,' Jas says, pointing.

She said 'Mum', thinks Clare.

'I sent a message to Pop, asking him what makes a special bird, and he sent this back.' She clicks on her grandfather's reply. *Well, all birds are special, except maybe pigeons and Indian mynas, but to me, a Hot Diggity bird is the feeling it gives you, Jasmine. You'll know it when you see it. The pale pygmy magpie goose gives you the Hot Diggities with a capital H. It's a Hot Diggity bird.*

'I'd like to see it if I could,' Jas says. 'And David seems harmless.'

Teenage girls, thinks Clare, can be the strangest, meanest, softest, sweetest things. He does seem harmless.

Jas goes to the sent mail list; there Clare sees pages of her father's messages to his granddaughter. 'How long were you sending him emails?'

'Since two Christmases ago. I started telling him about birds and stuff and then he wrote back. It was fun.'

'Why are you showing me these emails?'

'I want to see if Pop wrote anything about David Thomas from Melbourne. He said he sometimes liked to make notes of the birds he saw and the people he went birding with. I'm not *showing* you anything.'

Of course you're showing me something, Clare thinks. 'Well, just do a word search to check,' she says patiently.

Jas looks at the screen of the computer.

'Type in his name,' says Clare, feeling slightly awkward, 'and we'll see what your pop thought.'

Jas types in *David Thomas of Melbourne*. Up comes a document filled with dot-point paragraphs. One of the paragraphs has a highlighted name.

The day we saw the Gouldian: Gouldian finches have been captive finches. Beautiful birds. But any bird that's bred in captivity is a bird in a cage. In Nitmiluk National Park after dry season burn-off. Thought we'd get lucky. Went with David Thomas from Melbourne. We wandered around from mid-morning. Got late in the day. Thought we'd done with luck. David Thomas and I decide to head back to car and back to billet. David gets fidgety – realises he's left the captain's binoculars at little clump of trees on the west rise. He's so polite and apologises too many times. We go back to the clump. His captain's binoculars are there. Just before he picks them up he stops and says quietly, 'Tree to the right, there – three branches up.' And in a tree to the right, 4:00 pm, on a middle branch, is a Gouldian finch. Red-headed male. Hot Diggity. And a Hot Diggity is David Thomas of Melbourne.

That's the only mention of David on the computer.

'Hot Diggity . . .' says Clare, slowly.

'I always thought it was Hot *Dijity*,' says Jas. She pronounces the word with a 'j' sound, like didgeridoo. 'Are you sure that's not how you —'

'Well, google Perry Como and Hot Dijity and see for yourself.'

Jas types in the search box and up pops a number of video-clip options. Clare says, 'Go with the most plays.'

Jas opens a black and white video clip from the 1950s of grey-looking people – slick men in suits and women with tightly styled hair and big dresses, all making a hissing sound. Then one of the men starts singing.

Jas giggles again. 'Guess you're right – it's Diggity.'

They watch the video, listen to the aimless happy tune.

'Did Pop really sing this?'

Clare nods.

'That man looks nice,' says Jas. 'Sort of handsome in a harmless way.'

Perry Como pauses mid-smile as the song finishes.

Clare notices that the old agricultural magazine, yellow and dirty-looking, is lying on the desk. 'Did you bring that in?' she asks.

Jas nods. The laughter disappears from her face and she sits back and eyes her mother.

'Why did you bring it in here?' Clare hears herself in dismay. Why is she so annoyed and irritated?

'I just wanted to check,' says Jas.

'Check what? It's rubbish!'

Jas picks up the magazine and flips through the brittle pages to reveal an envelope tucked between two pages.

'I found this,' she says, and picks up the envelope – a long business one with a small oblong plastic window. It's from the Queensland State Lands Office. 'Look.'

Clare opens the envelope. Inside is a small greaseproof-paper-covered bundle. She takes it out and unwraps a collection of feathers: a small one of lime, splashed with electric blue and olive, another of emerald green, and the last one a brilliant azure. A small note is also enclosed.

On this day, 24 June 1950, I found these feathers. They are pretty. They remind me of you. One is a noisy pitta (not that you are noisy), one a large-tailed nightjar (which is a funny name for a pretty bird). My favourite is the blue of the azure kingfisher, a dressed-up fancy kookaburra. The colour is like your eyes. You have blue eyes and you sing very nice. I would like you to have these. My name is Tony. P.S. The Italian boy who sits by the far window in singing.

Clare looks at the note and then at the feathers. She carefully wraps up the little bundle again and puts it back in the envelope. Turning it over, she sees written quite neatly in an early attempt at running writing, *To Penny.*

Penny? Who could that have been? And why hadn't he given the parcel to her? Perhaps he was too shy. Perhaps he thought that an Italian boy who sat by the far window in singing couldn't hope for the chance to talk to Penny.

Clare looks down at the envelope; she can almost feel the hesitation, the excitement her father must have felt when he wrote these words, the sense of expectation. And then he would have taken it to school, and seen Penny, the girl he had collected these feathers for, seen her walking to school, or perhaps on a bus or in the playground.

Penny. Such an old Australian name. So different from Antonio, the Italian boy.

He would have walked towards her, holding the letter in his hands, feeling nervous, uncertain. Perhaps she looked at him and wondered what the Italian boy was doing. And he would have taken another step and then he would have felt that collapse in his chest. He would have turned away. And he would have felt his face burning. And Penny would have gone about her business. Or maybe, thinks Clare, maybe she wanted him to keep walking towards her, the Italian boy with the soft brown eyes. Maybe she wanted to know what that long cream envelope he held so gently in his hands contained.

Maybe.

She looks back at her daughter now, whose face is not angry or impassive or suspicious or accusatory but open.

'Why do you think he didn't give it to her?' Jas asks.

'I don't know, but I would have cried with happiness if someone had given this to me.'

'I would have cried, too,' says Jas.

Clare smiles down at her girl. 'Cried, "Hot Diggity"!'

'Or Dijity.'

'I'm sorry I thought this was on its way to the recycling. And I think I do need a hand in going through all this stuff.'

Jas waits.

'And I'll go and ask Mr Harmless if he'll take us birding tomorrow.'

'Us?' says Jas.

'Yes – us.'

'Good.' The girl sounds pleased.

Clare walks out the front door and around the verandah. The rain isn't far away, she thinks. As she turns the corner she hears the shower start. She is about to call to David to give him some warning when she catches a glimpse of him through a thinner patch of the bushes and pauses. His body is lit by the lamp, his back to her.

He touches the water and jumps back.

He tries again, then hops back even further. He swears a little, then she sees him. She hears him say, sternly, 'Come on, you silly bloody man.'

He makes another attempt to march into the shower but gets a few splashes on his arms and hops back, making a funny muffled yell. This tuns into a strangled scream, as he jumps into the air and kicks out with his foot. 'Go away, you bastard thing!' He must have landed on a toad, Clare thinks, stifling a laugh. As he flicks his foot his elbows rise up as if he is flapping his arms.

After having seen off the toad, he turns back to the falling water, takes a deep breath and walks back carefully some six steps, and then runs towards the water.

He's almost there but he swerves at the last moment.

He repeats this a few times until he simply stands still and then walks slowly into the running shower.

He steps under the water.

He's still for a moment and then explodes into frantic movement. 'Fuck, that's cold,' he exclaims. 'Fuck!'

Clare giggles.

David tenses his body and jumps and jogs on the spot, all the while whispering a strangled cry of 'Fuck fuck, fuck, fuck fuckark fuckark,' like some hybrid bird-man.

He lathers himself furiously with soap, which drops from his hand.

David turns around under the shower, grabs the soap he dropped and continues to lather. His eyes are closed, scrunched up as he repeats his birdman shower dance performance.

Clare suddenly realises she is staring at a naked man, full frontal, and makes herself sneak away, feeling naughty, but still giggly.

Harmless.

CHAPTER SIXTEEN

It is a good ten minutes after his shower before David's teeth stop chattering. Even now, as the last of the birders share their day's lists with the rest of the group, he can feel goosebumps on his arms. These are, David knows, a result of the freezing-cold water making the tiny muscles at the base of each hair contract and pull the hair erect. He knows this because a bearded Scottish vet had told him about goosebumps on a birding trip to Flinders Island in Bass Strait.

The vet was part of a mutton-bird research team, weighing and tagging chicks on the island. Their work in the field finished, the vet had joined a birding group of which David was a member. They had been on Flinders Island during the shearwater breeding season and to see the forty-spotted pardalote.

The birders had been divided into smaller groups and David and the vet were partnered for a day. Even though it was late November the temperatures were still only in the high single-figures and the wind was freezing.

After their day in the field, as he sat in the Furneaux Tavern, which overlooked the small harbour that serviced the southern end of the island, David couldn't quite believe how cold it had been.

Somebody had just put the old Kiss song 'I Was Made for Loving You' on the jukebox.

'Definitely a song for the younger set,' said the vet, before pulling at his drink and then at his beard. 'Do you know why goosebumps come about? Extremes, David, extremes. Cold weather or strong emotions like fear, euphoria or pleasure, sexual arousal or when you're about to get bitten on the arse by a leopard seal.

'Not just leopard seals, either – it could be any large sea mammal with big teeth,' he continued, after a pause. 'Well, it was freezing and I got frightened when I saw a seal in front of me so I tried to walk back as carefully as I could – very carefully – right into the mouth of another seal, which bit me on the bum.' He took another sip of his drink. 'Whether there was any hint of arousal when the thing sank in its fangs, I couldn't tell you. Another drink might help . . . but there was certainly a fair amount of fear and freezing weather.'

David had obliged, and the vet, nodding his head in thanks, carried on, 'The thing for you to figure out is whether you're cold, frightened or turned on. Maybe . . .' He pulled at his beard again. 'Maybe you're all three, David. And maybe I can help you,' he said, resting a very muscular hand upon David's thigh.

It came right out of the blue, or so it seemed to David. So he had sat, smiled, rather stupidly he thought, and tried to think what to do.

The vet didn't look at David for some time, but left his hand on David's thigh. Then he turned and looked into David's face. The vet's eyes were nervous and a little unsure; scared, thought David. Maybe he was emboldened by the booze, maybe just getting mixed signals. Maybe desperate, or just chancing his luck?

After a while, David had said politely, 'I think I'm just cold. Not frightened – flattered. But, you know . . .'

The vet had nodded, removed his hand, smiled back at David a little sadly and said, 'Well, you're a gent. No offence given, none taken. Winners all round.' His face flushed red and his eyes closed. Then, having barely missed a beat, he took a deep breath and carried on speaking, as if he had never put a searching hand under the table and on David's thigh. He spoke more about goosebumps, explaining that they were a part of the fight-or-flight response, in which an extreme emotion or sense makes an animal's muscles contract before it determines whether to stand its ground or flee.

David remembers the vet's words now as he half-listens to the birders in the lodge. The idea of an emotion, a strong emotion, causing the fight-or-flight reaction. In the case of love, he thought, 'fight' would be the embracing of love. And 'flight', then, the turning away and denying. Maybe that was what he had done to Genevieve Forti? Maybe it had been a case of polite flight?

It must be frightening, he thinks, to feel such an extreme emotion that the need to choose fight or flight was provoked. Perhaps he's never been provoked to that extent or perhaps he's been programmed to always choose a protective 'flight'; it might be set into his emotional DNA. To have to make that choice, thinks David, would be . . . interesting, which really isn't the right word.

Sitting in the lodge he thinks back to the vet in the tavern on Flinders Island, his hand on David's thigh, the look in his eyes. Would he describe that as 'interesting'? A lonely man, a quick grope under the table in a pub at the bottom of the world.

David tunes into his surroundings again as Clive Farquhar is saying something about curlews. 'Now, eastern curlews, of course, eastern curlews travel thousands of kilometres – thousands – just to find a mate. What some will do for a bit of company!'

David looks up at him and smiles absently. He thinks again of the vet, who must have travelled a long way, and might still be trying to find a bit of company. If that vet were a bird, thinks David, he'd be the bearded Scottish groper: travels to the bottom of the world for a quick fumble in the pub while a jukebox is playing 'I Was Made for Loving You'. What some people will do for a bit of company.

After the final birder has shared her list with the group, and the last of the Tim Tams have been sealed in a plastic container and popped into the fridge, the discussion turns to tomorrow's birding. Everyone agrees that the northern beaches and the mudflats would probably be the best place to start. However, they admit that there was never any certainty that the bird could be found; perhaps it's already gone back along its path of migration to Papua New Guinea.

'Just the luck of birding,' says Don Barrellon. 'Just the way things happen; can't force a bird to make itself findable. They have their way of doing things and they really don't give a fig about what we'd like to see.' He yawns and takes a few sips from his silver flask before bidding the other guests goodnight.

On his way out of the room, he walks over to David and drapes a hand over his shoulder. 'You look like you're miles away, David Thomas of Melbourne.'

David nods. 'Do you think birds – the migratory birds like Clive was talking about – know where their home is, Don?'

The big man sticks out his lower lip. 'How do you mean?'

'Well, like the pale pygmy magpie goose: it flies all the way down here to breed and then flies all the way back to Papua New Guinea.'

'So?'

'Well, where's its home? Here or Papua New Guinea or maybe somewhere else?'

Don thinks for a bit, tucks his lip back in. 'Well, who's to know with a bird? Maybe wherever the bird *is* is home,' he says, patting David's shoulder as he leaves. 'Odd thing to think about, David; most of us just want to see the bloody thing!'

Clare is still awake, waiting for David to come back from the lodge. She still has to ask him if it would be okay for her and Jas to go with him on the birding day tomorrow.

After seeing him shower dance, she had walked back into the study, to find Jas staring at the computer screen.

She had debated for a few moments whether or not to tell her daughter what she'd just seen, then decided against it and instead said, 'David Thomas of Melbourne has gone off to the birders' lodge; I'll ask him when he gets back.'

Jas, still focused on the computer, didn't reply.

'It might be time to shut the computer off now,' Clare had said, pleasantly enough.

Jas looked at her briefly and then back to the screen. More sternly: 'Jas, please turn that thing off now.' Then she realised Jas had been trying to turn it off. 'What have you been doing?' Clare asked.

Jas looked at her, eyes brimming with tears. Clare walked around to see what was on the screen, but her daughter stood up and tried to hold her back. Clare pushed past. On the screen was a collection of faces – postage-stamp-sized photos of men running down the length of the webpage.

Clare stared at the screen. Of all the things that could be accessed on the internet, she would never have believed that her teenage daughter would have led her to this: an online dating site. For the 'mature man'.

There before her was a random set of faces – old faces – accompanied by a sentence or two describing the sort of person to whom each face belonged. Most wore fleeces or polo shirts with their collars popped. They also wore uncertain smiles and comb-overs. Many of the shots seemed to have been taken on home computers, so the faces of the men had become distorted and compressed into strange shapes. Some have a hint of a smile, looking into the camera atop the computer screen, giving them an absent-minded, village-idiot gaze. Others wore the blank expressions of passport photos.

Clare stared – not blankly, but working herself in those few moments into the gaping feeling of wondering horror, thinking of every possible nightmare tabloid headline about sleazy internet traps and perversions before, finally, reaching an understanding of what she was looking at.

Then she heard Jas's voice. 'Who do you think I am? What do you think I'm doing?'

'I don't know, that's why I asked you.'

'I just —' Jas shrugged her shoulders.

'Why have you looked this up?'

'I didn't,' she snapped. 'It's a bookmark – a saved bookmark page.'

There is nothing quite like the scorn of a teenager when confronted by an adult trying to pass comment about a domain the teenager considers their own.

'Don't you talk to me like that!' Hearing her own voice Clare realised she was close to tears.

Jas turned to face her. She looked like she was about to cry too. 'He saved it. Pop saved it.'

Clare said, very slowly, 'What do you mean?'

'Oh God, Mum – just look for yourself.'

Clare had seen webpages like this before, when she was prompted by a friend after a wine to have a go on the net. 'Go on, see if you can find yourself an eBay boyfriend – you couldn't do any worse than the last one!'

Clare and her friend had laughed nervously, the alcohol helping as they scrolled through the rows of faces and read the few sentences provided under each one to give a reason why you should push a button for more contact. Some were like bumper-bar stickers: *Join me for life's journey. I'm all that I am and all that I am could be yours. Life is not forever but love can be.* Others sounded more like the names of law or accounting firms: *Affable and fit. Clean, broadminded and easy. Neat and loyal.* And all of them – well, almost all – liked walks along the beach, a bottle of red and *The Shawshank Redemption*. The bloody *Shawshank Redemption*! A film about men in prison who fall in love in that matey, manly way. It must have been some sort of lonely-guy brotherhood pledge or code, Clare had thought at the time, because so many included it in their list of likes. A film of true and enduring friendship and respect. Between men. There are no women in the film.

Even now, sitting with her daughter looking at a page of hapless old coots, Clare felt bewildered.

These would-be eBay boyfriends – or 'digital desperates', as Clare had thought of them – all cited it as their favourite film as they tried to find someone out there in internet land. Not one woman with any dialogue or even a name.

Clare looked at the screen in front of her, at the faces and their online names. 'Morefun68', 'taurus70', 'Fonz5', 'letsgo72', 'Manalone', 'Meeturdestinee' and then, halfway down the page, 'Funluva', a man with a ridiculous amount of hair who described himself as *well-read, tall, great teeth and lovely hands. Modest.* And above, 'Don64', a man whose photo looked like it came from a police charge sheet and who claimed to be *sincere, honest and compassionate and looking for a partner in crime.*

And there he was. Her father. He stared straight ahead, choosing the passport-photo approach. He went under the name of – what else? – 'HotDiggity'. Her father. She'd had no idea he had gone on a dating site. Well, why *should* she have known? Why *should* he have told her?

His sentence describing himself read, *I feel awkward doing this. But sometimes I am lonely.*

Clare looked at the screen and started crying. She could hear Jas crying, too.

'I thought it might be a bird thing,' her daughter sobbed.

But sometimes I am lonely. He had never said that to Clare. In all the conversations she had had with him over a phone line, whenever she asked, 'How's things?' he had always answered, 'Oh, thereabouts.'

Whenever she had sat on the verandah with him near his chest of Picnic reads, having cups of tea and blabbing on about where she was at in her life, he had never said to her, 'But sometimes I am lonely.'

When he had held her hand at the hospital and said to her, '*La mia bambina, la mia ragazza, mia dolce ragazza,*' he had never said, 'But sometimes I am lonely.'

She cried for that now and looked down at the desk to see the envelope containing the feathers. She turned to her daughter. 'Switch it off, baby,' she said slowly. 'Switch it off, *bambina*.'

Jas started closing down the site and then paused. 'You see what he saved it under?'

Clare looked to the top of the page: *Silly Old Man's first and only trip to Introduction Page (but not as silly as Strongwinds – third from top).*

Clare read it again. *Introduction Page*; nothing as forward as a dating site but an 'Introduction Page'. She followed her father's directions and scanned down the page again.

'Strongwinds64' had opted for the village-idiot look. He was sporting a wetsuit and holding, of all things, an axe. *I like the beach and the outdoors, am educated, can do a cartwheel. Have own teeth and hair. And prosthetic limb.*

She looked at Hot Diggity's photo again. It wasn't just another face; if you looked closely you could see there was something in his eyes, a hint of a smile. He'd taken it at this computer, the messy bookshelves there in the background, looking just as they did now.

'Do you think anyone answered him?' asked Jas.

'Don't know, but I bet he did a lot better than old Strongwinds64.'

'But why did he do it?'

Clare took a breath. 'He did it because he wanted to. It was his business. And even though he was lonely sometimes, it looks like he had a bit of fun. Now turn it off, turn off Hot Diggity's computer.'

Jas did as she was told and went to bed with a polite moroseness, which Clare thankfully accepted over more unpredictable teenage passion or angst.

Clare got up and went outside to wait for David Thomas.

She stands for a while on the verandah. It is quite something, she thinks, to find out a little of the life that your father lived. First the feathers in the envelope, then the dabbling in the world of cyber relationships.

Why it should shock her, she doesn't know. Looking through the contents of her father's computer isn't that different from going through the boxes and files of his belongings. Ollie, as executor, had gone through their father's diaries and ledgers. The house is full of bits and pieces of a life that is only now being revealed to her.

Clare decides that another glass of wine will help, so heads for the kitchen, but when Picnic lets out a cry she stops and leans down to the chest instead.

'All right, bird, a biscuit and a story or two,' she says, and reaches into the chest, pulling out the collected Picnic reads that her father had compiled in the scrapbook.

First she reads a Kenneth Slessor poem called 'The Night-Ride', the story of a train journey and a passenger waking at a country station as if in a dream.

Gas flaring on the yellow platform; voices running up
  and down;
Milk-tins in cold dented silver; half-awake I stare,
Pull up the blind, blink out – all sounds are drugged;
The slow blowing of passengers asleep;
Engines yawning; water in heavy drips;
Black, sinister travellers, lumbering up the station,
One moment in the window, hooked over bags;
Hurrying, unknown faces – boxes with strange labels –
All groping clumsily to mysterious ends,
Out of the gaslight, dragged by private Fates.
Their echoes die. The dark train shakes and plunges;
Bells cry out; the night-ride starts again.
Soon I shall look out into nothing but blackness,

Pale, windy fields. The old roar and knock of the rails
Melts in dull fury. Pull down the blind. Sleep. Sleep.
Nothing but grey, rushing rivers of bush outside.
Gaslight and milk-cans. Of Rapptown I recall nothing
  else.

She likes the last line especially, so much that she reads the whole poem again.

Then, turning the page, she sees Wordsworth's 'I Wandered Lonely as a Cloud'.

She laughs a little. 'Oh, come on, Dad. Hot Diggity does the Romantic poets?' But she feeds the bird a bit of biscuit and settles down to read the poem.

Her father had marked the last passage in the poem as being 'beautiful, just beautiful'.

For oft, when on my couch I lie
In vacant or in pensive mood,
They flash upon that inward eye
Which is the bliss of solitude;
And then my heart with pleasure fills,
And dances with the daffodils.

She thinks for a moment and reads the poem again, smiling.

CHAPTER SEVENTEEN

David walks as quietly as he can along the verandah to where he left his swag by the chest, not wanting to disturb Clare or her daughter. He would have quite liked to see Clare again but isn't sure what he would be interrupting.

He edges past a collection of eskies and some bracketed wooden tennis racquets and then stops, hearing something – a voice, perhaps. There are still some fruit bats hooning around in the trees but it's not those that stop him. *Is* it a voice? Then a laugh. He knows that laugh. It's her. Clare.

David peers carefully around the corner of the verandah. And sees her. It is Clare, sitting down in profile to him under the yellowish light in which bugs are zipping around.

She's in the chair near the chest, and she's reading aloud. 'That inward eye which is the bliss of solitude.'

Standing just in front of her is the stone curlew, looking at her expectantly. Clare speaks again and David turns his head so he can hear better.

'That is beautiful,' she says, and resumes reading.

David realises that he knows the poem. It's the one about the flowers, about the daffodils. He can't stop himself from reciting it aloud too: 'And then my heart with pleasure fills, And dances with the daffodils.'

Clare starts and the curlew cries.

David steps out from around the corner, half-apologetic but also a little excited; he heard what she was saying and she's a fair distance from him. And, he thinks, it's Clare.

'I'm sorry,' he says.

'Jesus, how long were you there for?'

'Just for the last bit of the poem. The daffodil poem.'

She looks at him with her wide eyes. He looks back and apologises again.

'It's all right,' says Clare. 'As a matter of fact I was waiting for you.'

'For me?'

'Yes,' she says, pausing a little before continuing, 'David Thomas of Melbourne.'

He smiles. It is a nice smile.

Clare thinks for a moment of him dancing under the cold shower. 'Yes, I was.'

'Well, how can I help?' He feels the slight prickle of goosebumps. It might still be the cold, but he doubts it.

'I'm sorry about before. It's been all go here with the birders turning up yesterday and then you come and deliver my daughter, so you know . . .'

He gestures with his hands in a placating way. 'Yes, sorry about that. She looks like you – your daughter.'

'Yes, I heard you say that to Neil.'

He nods. 'Old birder's trick to try to help identify a species and type – watch how birds move and hold themselves. It's the jizz.'

'The jizz?'

He nods again. He's pretty sure his goosebumps aren't because of the cold. Rain is beginning to fall. Only a few drops, but heavy ones.

Picnic cries out again.

'All right, Picnic, just wait.'

'Why is she called Picnic?'

'I don't know. She was my dad's pet or something like that. Neil presented her to me. Said she wasn't quite right.'

David looks at the bird, which has turned to face him with an almost imperceptible movement. He can see that one wing isn't right and the beak isn't formed properly.

'So my dad looked after it. I never knew anything about it until Murph dropped it off.'

'Well, Neil is full of secrets,' says David and, feeling a little guilty, adds, 'but then most people are.'

Clare nods. She's silent for a while and then says something softly. He thinks it's 'yes'.

'You said you were waiting for me?' he asks.

'Yes,' she says.

'And you were filling in time by reading poetry to the bird?'

'Picnic.'

'Sorry, by reading poetry to Picnic.'

'How long did you say you were standing around the corner?'

He can feel his goosebumps again. 'Well, I didn't want to disturb anybody and then I thought I heard something and then I realised it was you and you were —' He stops. 'You were reading Wordsworth,' he says at last, 'to Picnic, who happens to be a stone curlew with a dodgy wing and a cleft beak.'

'As you do on an evening in North Queensland.'

'As you do,' he says.

'I was wondering whether it would be all right if, and you can say no, if Jas – my daughter – and I . . .' She pauses and does a clicking thing with her fingers. 'If we might come along with you for a bit. Tomorrow, while you're out looking for your bird.'

Would it be okay? Would it? He'll have to share a car with Neil or one of the other birders. Is it okay for two more to come along? He isn't quite sure.

Clare asks again in a louder voice, taking him a bit by surprise. 'Sorry,' she says, 'I wasn't quite sure whether you heard me.'

He looks at her then he thinks a bit. 'Have you been raising your voice when you speak to me?'

She nods.

'How did you know?'

'Your jizz – an old teacher's trick.'

'But I heard you from around the corner when you were reading the Wordsworth.'

'Yes, the Wordsworth,' she says.

'If you come with me tomorrow, do you mind racing about a little? I'd like to try and see the bird.'

The rain is getting a little heavier.

'Of course. That's why Jas wants to go. It's why she came here, I think. Because of the bird.'

He looks at her.

'Your special bird. She has a thing for them, I think. Not just your pale pygmy but birds in general.'

'Good. Good.' He smiles. 'Do you have a thing for birds?'

'No, not really.'

'Then why read Wordsworth poems to them?'

'It's not just Wordsworth,' Clare says, 'there was one by Philip Larkin and another by Kenneth Slessor. My dad,' she explains. 'I think my dad used to read them to Picnic. Well, maybe as much to himself as to the bird. But he left a chest here full of Picnic reads. And you know, Picnic is a good audience.'

'I like that poem, the flower poem.'

She looks at him but doesn't say anything.

David looks at the bird and then out at the rain. 'It's a real birder's poem, I think. You know, you see something that you think is pretty remarkable – like the daffodils after you've floated across the landscape – and you don't really know just how beautiful a thing it is you've seen. Maybe you never will, maybe you've been after a particular bird, something you've set your heart on seeing, and because you don't find it, you never appreciate what you've been a part of.' He stops and listens to the rain for a while. 'But sometimes when you're alone, you remember, and then, if you're lucky and have that blissful solitude, then you . . .' He laughs. 'You get goosebumps.' There is a pause. 'God, I sound like a wanker.'

'Sort of, but in a good way,' Clare responds, looking back out to the rain.

'Does Picnic just like poetry? Or did your dad have other things to offer as well?'

'There's a chestful of stuff, David Thomas of Melbourne. The first thing I read was a James Bond book.'

'James Bond?'

'Yeah, my dad had marked out passages. He even kept score of a golf game they were having.'

'*Goldfinger!* You read *Goldfinger* to the curlew. To Picnic, I mean.'

Now Clare is not so sure about David Thomas; he seems a little too enthusiastic about *Goldfinger*. 'You know it?' she asks.

'Know it! God, it's one of the all-time great bad books. Great when you're a thirteen-year-old boy with a face covered in acne but then if you read it again when you're forty it's gloriously awful.'

'You know about Pussy Galore?'

'And the stirring in the loins at the sight of a beautiful lesbian?'

Clare smiles.

David stares at her. He knows he's staring but he doesn't care. And he thinks she doesn't either.

'Do you have the book out here?' he asks suddenly.

She nods.

'Do you mind if I read the last page? I bet your father marked it.'

Clare finds the book, looks inside and passes it to David. There is a single exclamation mark running down the final page.

David sits in the camp chair on the other side of the small table and begins to read out loud about fishermen's jumpers being decent to get around in by half an inch and black commas of hair falling over Bond's eyes and special treatment reserved for beautiful lesbians who can't run as fast as an uncle. Of a face that suddenly wasn't that of a criminal and, yes, not even a lesbian, but of that most basic of things, apparently – a woman who just wants to be made to feel like she matters by a man who knows how to make a woman like that matter.

The last paragraph reads like a sports commentator describing someone eating at a restaurant, with eyeballs being kissed and mouths coming down savagely on bits and pieces of anatomy.

Picnic tilts her head to one side and then the other as David reads. When he has finished, he and Clare both laugh while Picnic cries and Clare throws her a piece of biscuit.

Clare is still for a moment then asks, 'Why did you read *Goldfinger* again?' She placed an incredulous emphasis on *again*.

David looks at the bird, the book and finally at Clare. 'Birding trip in Tasmania. Pouring rain. Twelve people in a lodge for nearly three days. The library wasn't that big so I got to meet Goldfinger again.' He smiles. 'What else did he have in there?'

'All sorts of stuff,' Clare says. 'Books on engineering and pages torn from all sorts of things – one from *The Moon and Sixpence*, about someone who bore a startling resemblance to Somerset Maugham leaving an island in the South Pacific and waving goodbye to the landlady of the boarding house where he'd been staying while seeking the banker who became an impressionist painter on the jetty and felt somehow closer to death.'

She pats the chest. 'There's bits and pieces of all sorts in here.'

'May I?' asks David, and Clare nods. He picks up a manila folder with the words 'Something for Picnic from across the Tasman' written across the front in Tony Cirillo's careful hand.

David opens the folder and looks at the page that is clipped inside.

'What is it?' asks Clare.

'A poem.'

'Well . . . ?'

'Well what?'

'Well, read it.'

David coughs and then starts reading aloud. '"Waterfall" by a woman called Lauris Edmond.

I do not ask for youth, nor for delay
In the rising of time's irreversible river
That takes the jewelled arc of the waterfall
In which I glimpse, minute by glistening minute,
All that I have and all I am always losing
As sunlight lights each drop fast, fast falling.

I do not dream that you, young again,
Might come to me darkly in love's green darkness
Where the dust of the bracken spices the air
Moss, crushed, gives out an astringent sweetness
And water holds our reflections
Motionless, as if for ever.

It is enough now to come into a room
And find the kindness we have for each other
– calling it love – in eyes that are shrewd
But trustful still, face chastened by years
Of careful judgement; to sit in the afternoons
In mild conversation, without nostalgia.

But when you leave me, with your jauntiness
Sinewed by resolution more than strength
– suddenly then I love you with a quick
Intensity, remembering that water,
However luminous and grand, falls fast
And only once into the dark pool below.

Neither says anything as the rain falls.

'That's quite lovely,' says Clare.

David nods. 'There's a bit more – that your dad added.' He holds it out to Clare, who takes it and looks down at her father's writing. She feels that familiar pang of recognition.

'It would be nice, Picnic – it would be lovely – if I could share this . . . this realisation with somebody once more,' she reads aloud. She doesn't know whether David is looking at her and she doesn't know why she would care. 'New Zealanders,' she says suddenly. 'New Zealanders have a thing for waterfalls.' And she drops the folder back in the chest.

'I suppose it's good to have a thing for something.'

'Maybe,' says Clare impassively.

He can think of nothing to say in response and looks at Picnic. Then, 'I bet you he had the curlew poem by Kath Walker,' says David.

'By who?'

'Kath Walker – "The Curlew Cried". She's an Indigenous poet.'

'Who?' says Clare.

David looks at her and then smiles slightly. 'By Oodgeroo . . .' He pauses, trying to remember.

'Noonuccal,' finishes Clare. 'And it is indeed here.'

'That's a beautiful poem.'

'You're just saying that because it's about a bird.'

'Well, maybe. But it's a beautiful poem. And honest.'
He stops for a moment. 'Curlews. We were talking about
them before in the lodge. How they travel thousands of
kilometres.'

'Not Picnic.'

'No. Not poor old Picnic. I've always wondered where
a bird like that – a migratory bird – would feel at home.'

There is a silence.

'Where do you feel at home, David Thomas of
Melbourne?'

'I don't know. I love Melbourne. I grew up there. Don't
really want to move away. As well as birds, there's the footy,
ACMI, the MCG, the lanes, the hot-soup-and-crumpet
cosiness, the State Library. But, you know . . . it's not like I
particularly want to stay, either. I come here and I remember,
I feel things that make me think *this* is my home. And I
feel that way in lots of other places too.'

They listen to the rain for a little while.

'Do you have a . . .' Clare can't finish the question.
She feels herself going red. Come on, ask him. Are you in
a relationship? Do you have a girlfriend, a wife, a lover?
But she can't.

He didn't hear. Thank Christ.

David looks at Clare. He thinks she may have said
something, but he's not sure. He waits a bit. Nothing.

'Well, I know I've got to fly home tomorrow. This was it. I'm completely broke and they won't forgive another AWOL at work. I've got nothing apart from this job.'

'Nothing?' she asks. She can't quite believe it.

'Nothing.' He thinks. 'Well, a mattress, three weeks' rent, fifty books about birds, a collection of textas and my MCC membership.'

'Jesus, that's not "nothing"!'

He looks at her.

'An MCC membership? Like, *all* the cricket and *all* the football? In the members'?' Clare says.

David nods.

'I've been in the members' once. Once.'

'I know. Spoilt. I would have given it up if I could a few times. It's five hundred dollars a year. Luckily, I couldn't do that to Mum.'

'Does she pay your fees or something?'

'No, Mum died a while ago. She just loved the members'. Mad Melbourne supporter. We were all signed up at birth.'

'Ah, so that's why.'

He nods. 'Who do you go for?'

'Who do you think?'

'I don't know, but I would like you to be a Richmond supporter.'

Picnic cries and Clare gives the bird another biscuit. 'Why?'

'They have a great team song.' He starts singing it; after a few phrases Clare joins in. They finish off with, 'Yellow and black.'

'You're right. It is a good song but I'm a Collingwood supporter.'

He looks at her.

'I know – beautiful bird but awful team.' She laughs. 'No, you're right. I'm from Tigerland.'

Her smile, her smile is – what? He suddenly feels prickles on his arms. Her smile is something that will flash upon his inner eye that is the bliss of solitude. He turns away. This is not something that should be happening. He turns back; she's speaking.

'I think I know what you mean. Being up here, I feel my timetable is changing. Before, rising at five would mean a jetlag hangover, needing as much carbohydrate to get through as a real hangover. Now, it feels natural to see the dawn.' She looks at him, thinking of the shower dance. She hides a grin and then looks at his eyes. They are nice, too. She's frowning and she knows it but she can't help herself.

David looks at her. For an attractive woman she wears a serious frown, but a part of him realises he quite likes that.

'What's your favourite movie?' she asks suddenly.

'Well, apart from *Goldfinger* . . .'

She laughs.

'This'll sound a bit random but, well . . . I used to like *Chitty Chitty Bang Bang* because for some reason whenever we went to the movies as kids it was always to that one. And my parents sang along to it, to this one song about the car, I remember. And they were always singing out of tune, like they did at the football. And we always got Choc Tops.'

She's still looking at him, waiting.

'Didn't mind *Jaws* and *Star Wars*, too, I suppose,' he offers.

Clare feels vaguely embarrassed that she's amused that he had listed movies about a flying car, a killer shark and light sabres as his favourites. She can't help herself. 'What about *The Shawshank Redemption*?'

He thinks for a moment. 'The one about the prison? Jesus!' he exclaims. 'Well, I suppose it was okay. Bloody long, though.'

She laughs more enthusiastically than he expects. 'And you know what else I love about being here? The delicious-ness of an afternoon nap. From Melbourne, where it seems a crime to be indoors – even to see a movie – if the sun's out, to here, where the heat and sun are such a given that being in a dark room during the day is an acceptable pleasure. And to wake in the late afternoon, the sun sneaking through the slats of the blinds, everything golden . . .'

David looks at her face, animated and luminous under the verandah light. She's happy, he thinks, and Clare throws a bit of biscuit to the bird.

David looks at Picnic who's trying to manage with the crumb, her eyes staring back at him. A very unusual bird, he decides.

'The other thing about birds like Picnic – a stone curlew – is that they always have the same mate. Always. Somebody at the lodge tonight, when we were talking about curlews, said it's funny what lengths they travel to find a mate and stay together. Funny bird.'

Clare thinks of her father, of that envelope and of Hot Diggity on the website, of what *people* will do to find a mate. Then she remembers the newspapers in the chest of Picnic reads. 'I might have something else to read to the bird.'

David watches as she rummages about in the chest and pulls out copies of the local paper, all opened to the same section. It's just below the public notices, a good half page under the heading 'Meeting Point'. Her father had marked some of his favourites and added how many times they had appeared. Maybe he had originally been searching for something else there as he read them out to the bird, but she can see that his interest in the personal columns crossed over all categories.

She gives a couple of copies to David and there under the yellow light they read some of the highlighted entries. Almost all the men in the ads were unbelievably picky, wanting slim, fit, non-smoking ladies, while the one defiant woman-seeking-gent described herself as 'Athletic, outdoorsy and a sporty non-smoker. Weighs 95 kilograms,' Clare reads aloud.

'Good for her,' says David.

Another couple catch Clare's attention and she reads them out for David's benefit. '"Are you lonely and seeking companionship? Why not buy a galah? Phone Bob." "Sixty-five-year-old, almost impotent, willing to try the other side. Am genuine and very curious. Nothing too big."

'That is sort of a tragicomedy,' Clare says, giggling. '"Almost Impotent" sounds like a bad racehorse!' She smiles, then says, 'I can't believe how much this area must have changed for my father since he grew up here.' She thinks of the shy Italian boy who used to sit next to the window in singing.

David reads out the last entry in 'Male seeking male': '"Fifty-five, fit, healthy. Very sporty. Many tatts and loves wearing ladies' lingerie." I don't know why I'm laughing,' he says. 'It's not like I've had a charmed life of lasting relationships.' He looks to Clare. She has turned away to look at the rain.

He's a nice man, she thinks. And there is a confused feeling inside her – of broken homes and tears and wanting to feel something and not being able to.

'If you were to put an entry into the local paper's meeting point ads, what would you write?' he asks.

Clare looks at him and back out to the rain. He's trying to be nice. 'Grumpy girl seeks gorgeous boy. No axe murderers need apply.'

She says it so slowly and simply, he can't do anything but laugh.

Clare closes her eyes. His lovely laugh.

The rain continues to fall.

David sits, thinking. The rain could mean anything. It might wash out all hope of the bird being spotted. It might freshen the lagoons and the mudflats. But he doesn't care. He has goosebumps. He takes a breath and speaks. 'I may be a nerdy birder, but I'm not an axe murderer. And I'm not particularly gorgeous, but I don't think you're that grumpy. Really.'

She turns back to him. He looks into her eyes.

And then . . .

She stands and says, 'Goodnight.' And Picnic cries.

CHAPTER EIGHTEEN

David is up before dawn. He slept well enough. Considering. He kept thinking about her. He sees the heavy rain has become a drizzle. The day could go either way. He packs the few things not already in his swag and heads out in the darkness. He hears a morning bird call and listens; he can't resist. He reaches for his binoculars and creeps around to the front of the house, from where the bird is calling. A dove or pigeon call.

He finds it, a topknot pigeon. He watches it as the sky lightens a little, a thin shaft of light casting a halo around the tree. An aura. He smiles; this place is unbelievable. He turns to go back to his swag. As he is making his way around the verandah, a light suddenly goes on inside. Clare is standing there, looking out. She shows no sign of having noticed David in the dark. David stays still, reluctant to move in case she sees him. He feels like a peeping Tom. Clare moves towards her chest of drawers and, in one smooth movement, lifts her singlet over her head. David tries to look away, but fails. Her profile is beautiful, her skin looks soft and inviting, even from this distance. Her breast shaped beautifully. Unable to stop himself, David gives her a score of ten out of ten. They are his favourite kind of breasts. Even as he thinks it he is telling himself that his behaviour is awful. He is treating her like an object, but . . . God, he thinks, I want her.

Clare turns face-on and bends to pick up her bra from the end of the bed.

David is shocked. In place of one of her breasts there is only a line. From where her breast should begin to swell in her cleavage to under her arm is a thick, harsh, purple, bumpy, badly drawn scar.

Before David can compute what that means, Clare lifts her bra, reorganising something within one cup. She puts it on. She has two breasts. She pulls on a clean T-shirt and turns back to the dresser.

Without thinking further, his head confused, feeling ashamed, David scuttles awkwardly along the tree line to the front of the house. He steps down from the verandah, his feet making the timber squeak slightly, and then onto the gravel path that leads to the orchard and the lodge. The gravel makes a crunching sound but he walks quickly along the path and then through the gate to the orchard, away.

In her bedroom, Clare hears soft footsteps on gravel, the gate to the orchard closing, and waits until she can't tell if what she's hearing is the sound of footsteps, silence, the fridge in the kitchen, or the wind gently stirring in the trees.

She manages to extract a groan from Jas the third time she tries to wake her up. She can see that Jas had readied a backpack the night before so at least she had the intention of going out birding. It was just that the reality of an early start, the teenage love of a sleep-in and the weariness from her travels are now conspiring against her.

Clare has just come back in, having gone out to the verandah to find the swag already packed and no sign of David. She stood out there alone, listening to the sounds of early morning, before walking back inside.

Now, she looks down at Jas, who tries to pull the blankets back up and turns away from Clare, curling herself into a little ball. Clare fears Jas has inherited all the bad aspects of her own character. She's worried as well about not always being there to help her, her own mother having died when Clare was twenty-eight.

Soon after that Clare thought she should get married, have babies. In hindsight she realised she had probably pushed Gary into it – not that he wasn't willing. Would she have chosen him if she hadn't felt that compulsion? Would she ever have chosen anyone? Looking back, it seems as if she had never chosen, not really. She had jumped thoughtlessly from one lover, house or job to another without ever maintaining a self that could be alone – that could be strong and alone, could take time and think. Just, *Oh my god, he likes me! I'm in love! I'm there.* Or, *What a great house, cool people, I'm there!* Or, worst of all, the politeness hostage. *Sure, I'll move in and help pay the rent even though I'm not sure I like you that much and I know I don't like your friends or your politics.*

Then last night, for the first time that she can remember, she had spent time with a man and enjoyed herself. Enjoyed him, listening to him. Enjoyed that he seemed to like being there, too. And when he had stared at her, she had felt warm and had wanted him to – what?

I wanted him to kiss me.

She feels warmth now, at the memory. But she knows

that when she feels desire, her body won't behave as she wants it to.

Sitting on the edge of her daughter's bed, she feels a rush of anger at the things boyfriends had done to her in the past: pregnancy panics – a dash to get the morning-after pill when the guy hadn't even cared enough to come with her. Said he'd put the coffee on but was still farting in her bed when she got home. Getting warts from another boyfriend who'd had one last root with a former girlfriend for old times' sake and then come back with a present for Clare.

And then she thought about her body. Having to have a complete diathermy that made her susceptible to cervical cancer. Clare pauses in her stream of thoughts. Now, feeling dry and empty and harsh.

Here beside her is her daughter, mad one minute, clingy the next, mixed up by how her body is changing and how she is leaving behind the land of childhood. Clare worries about not being able to protect Jas from those ups and downs and roundabouts in life, the dumb decisions made out of fear or boredom or to spite someone. She knows she probably shouldn't even try, but hopes she will be around to share them with her daughter, as much as any mother can.

And then she feels it. Clare knows that sick dull fear at the thought of leaving her daughter, and the way it pulls at her with a relentlessness that confuses and angers her. She strokes Jas's head. 'Oh my little girl. I love you so.'

Jas flicks away her mother's hand and says grumpily, 'All right. All right, I'm up. Getting up.' She is on early morning autopilot and clearly hasn't heard Clare's words. She might as well have been an alarm going off.

Jas saved time in getting ready for the day by sleeping in her birding clothes and now she fumbles with her boots.

'There's no need to rush, Jas. I don't know where David has gone; he might come back a bit later for us.'

Jas rubs her eyes and looks at her mother. 'What, did you scare him off as well?'

Clare doesn't say anything; how can she? It's what she thought, too, when she saw the packed swag. She doesn't think 'scared' is the right word, though – maybe 'pissed' is more apt. Pissed off. Or bored. Or . . . something, just something.

There is a knock at the front door.

David got as far as the bottom of the first orchard before he stopped. He wondered whether to walk down to the side gate and head to the lodge. If he went to the lodge he'd get caught up in the final preparations for the day's twitch.

He stood, knowing he didn't want to do that; he wanted to go back to the house. So he had turned and then swore. He stood there and flapped his hands a bit. It was just a chance he might see the bird. Neil thought it had probably already left.

He looked back through the orchard to the house. Great, he thought, I want to go back there *why*? I said I'd take them birding. It's only polite and I have to get my swag. And I want to see her, to explain. Explain what? *I saw you through your window*? Christ, he thought. I didn't *mean* to see. Yes, that will be good. In my birding gear and binoculars and floppy hat I stood outside your window just before dawn.

Dawn. The chorus was starting; he could hear bits of song. He couldn't think about what he might be missing. If he held his head a certain way the sounds seemed to have more clarity. There, he could make out a catbird. Well, anyone could recognise that, but he could also hear a golden whistler and a rufous fantail, a kookaburra. And – and the vehicles from the lodge driving off.

He swore again. He'd have to go to the house now. He had one last try at hearing the emerging day, holding his head in the position that seemed to work best. It was then that he saw it, in the dawn light, a feather lying not far from his foot. He moved forward, still holding his head on an angle to pick up the birdsong, and walked straight into the branch of a fruit tree. It hit him on the bridge of his nose, sticking out from beneath his floppy hat, and knocked his head back. He yelled, more in fright than anything else. Thinking he could feel blood he touched his left eye.

He walked through the orchard, dodging trees like a drunken man grasping for a railing, then back up to the verandah. He stood at the door and knocked.

Standing back, he sees a splodge of blood on the door where he knocked. He goes to wipe it off with his hanky but the door opens.

Clare opens the door just as a hanky-clad palm moves towards her. She yells. The hand retracts.

'Sorry! It's me. David. David Thomas.'

Clare stands back.

'Sorry!' David says again. 'I just walked into a tree branch and cut my head and I knocked on your door. Left a bit of blood.'

Clare opens the door fully and sees that he is bleeding. 'Are you all right?'

'Um. Sort of . . .'

'It was just —'

'Yes, sorry.'

'No – well, it was a bit like being attacked by a Muppet.'

David looks at his hanky. A Muppet. He smiles.

Clare ushers him down the hall and through to the bathroom.

Jas comes out of her room. 'So you didn't scare him off?' She looks more closely at David. 'Did you hit him?'

Clare ignores her daughter.

'What were you doing?' Jas asks David.

'Couldn't resist trying to see some birds and I ended up in the orchard. And said good morning to a branch.'

'The top orchard? Would've been a lemon tree that got you.'

Clare looks at her daughter as she sits David down on the lip of the bath. 'How do you know that?' she asks.

'The bottom orchard was sour citrus – lime and grape-fruit – and the middle orchard was sweet citrus. Pop showed me last Christmas. The top orchard has the big, old lemon trees growing in it.'

David remembers the feather he found and goes to pat his top pocket to make sure it's still there. As he does so he brushes his hand against Clare's left breast. Or whatever it is that is where the left breast used to be.

'Sorry,' he says instinctively.

Clare looks back at him and reddens. She asks Jas to get some Dettol and Rawleigh's that she had packed back into the cabinet.

'Sorry,' says David again.

'It's all right.'

'What's Rawleigh's, Mum?'

'The stuff in the gold tin.'

Jas rummages through the shelves and brings out a collection of tins. She looks on as Clare cleans David's wound. 'There's a lot of tins,' she says and then, as an afterthought, 'Does this mean we're not going birding?'

David winces a little. 'Well, I hope not.'

'Jas, can you give us a tin, please?'

There is no reply. Clare asks again and Jas puts down the tin she was holding and hands her mother another. She walks out with a couple more of the tins and disappears down the hall.

'Jas?' Clare stops herself from calling out again and takes a moment before applying some salve to David's head. 'She obviously doesn't do mornings.'

David's eye line is directly at Clare's breasts. Well, breast. He tries to turn his head away.

She stops him. 'Just keep still. It's not that bad – a dressing and some sticking plaster should do you.'

He feels ashamed and foolish. And he likes how she smells. Oh my God, he thinks, and drops his head.

'What's the matter? Just be still.' Clare sounds cranky.

'Awfully awkward,' he mumbles.

Clare stands back, opens her arms wide and gestures with her hands. 'What *is* the problem?'

He looks up at her and is about to say something when he feels how tight the bandage is on his forehead. He raises his eyebrows and twists his head a bit.

She looks down at him and frowns.

'It's a bit tight, just feels a bit odd, but thank you,' he says uncertainly.

Clare bites her lip. It does look tight, and his eyelid and forehead are stretched, as if he's had a bad facelift like one of those horror stories from the shiny trashy magazines. Perhaps she should take it off, start again? But then he moves his head again; bugger him, she thinks, he was moving about when she tried to put it on, and it's five thirty in the morning. And he was the idiot wandering about in the dark. She looks at him as he makes his funny face again.

David thinks he should try to explain. Just explain how he felt. How he – shit, how he thought. He shakes his head. 'I'm sorry, Clare, I —'

'It's all right.'

'No, look, I shouldn't be going on. It's . . . as I went out walking this morning, coming around on the verandah, I tried to be as quiet as possible and I didn't mean to look . . .'

She stares back at him, impassive. Yes, impassive is the word, he thinks.

And she looks at him, and her eyes are lovely.

'Your light went on and I was . . . I could see, and I'm sorry.'

He saw me, realises Clare.

'And I feel very embarrassed and I'm sorry.'

He saw me.

'And . . .'

Clare closes her eyes and tries to think of nothing.

'And I . . .'

She can't help herself. 'Why were you embarrassed?'

'Because I really liked – well, you looked lovely. And then when I saw you,' he gestures with his hand to the left-hand side of his own chest. 'When I saw what you had obviously been through, what you —' Christ, he thinks. 'Look, you've had your breast removed and I felt ashamed because I saw that and I know it must be awful and . . . personal and I don't know why I'm telling you this because I don't really know you and . . .' He just stops.

She has opened her eyes and is looking at him.

Don't say anything, he tells himself. And then he hears his voice. 'But you did look really nice.'

It has been a while since Clare has heard any complimentary words. And even if she did have to decipher a fair amount of what he said, there is something of value in nice words.

'Oh well, I'll give you the benefit of the doubt; you've just walked into a dead lemon tree.' And then, surprising herself, she hears her own voice. 'It makes us even, David Thomas of Melbourne. I saw you under the shower.'

He looks confused.

'As you did your shower dance. Back and front.'

'Well, we've both given a display – unknowingly.' He smiles a little. 'Just like two albatrosses. An idiosyncratic process, unique to that type of bird.'

'What? A mating display?'

'Well, look, I was just trying to be funny and, I don't know, sometimes a display is not just about mating. It's just a display to see if there's any interest, you know, throwing it out there?' David is doing his best. 'I'm sorry. I'm sorry if you're not attracted to this particular albatross.'

'It's not that.'

David tries to just sit.

Clare can feel a mixture of annoyance, running to anger and something else, something like warmth. 'It's confusing. It's not that you seem to be some freak who goes to extreme lengths to perve and satisfy his one-breasted-woman thing. You might be trying to be honest and you made a bad joke but it's that same old thing – that man thing.'

'The man thing?'

'Bad jokes about mating, about sex.' She turns away and continues, 'Where do men get their natural bloody arrogance? All that stuff about "poor boys", and girls doing better at school, making boys feel useless and unheard and – Christ. When was it that men didn't rule the world? When in my life have men had it bad compared to women?'

'*That's* the man thing?'

'Now you'll hate me because I'm a feminist bitch. And I would like to be a feminist bitch, and I want to be angry and throw teapots. But we're not allowed to anymore. What happened to the lovely Irish girl with a temper being attractive, or the fiery Italian woman? When did it change to all the wild boys wanting bread-baking earth mothers? Thin ones. Since when do baking and skinny fit together?' She knows she's going over the top, notices David is smiling. 'Are you smiling? Are you laughing at me?'

'It was pretty funny.'

'How dare you laugh at me!'

'Sorry. Sorry.' David struggles to regain a straight face, or as straight a face as he can with one side of his face stretched out of shape. He gestures for her to carry on.

Clare looks at him, then looks away, burying her head in her hands. Fuck him, she thinks. Fuck him; fuck every fuck in the world. Who was the stupid person who said 'fuck' was a powerful word? If it were powerful, once would do. Twice in emergencies. But everyone who says 'fuck' says it *all the fucking time*! She feels laughter bubble in her guts. She tries to repress it but her body starts to shake, her shoulders . . . Behind her hands her smile is wide. She feels David touch her gently.

'I'm so sorry.' David thinks she is crying.

Clare lifts her hands away for a moment, and then realises she may be crying, she can't tell. Even in her hysteria, she can feel the Clare outside of herself judging her. The Clare who feels ridiculous when trying to have a good cry. Outside Clare thinks, Ah, so this is hysteria, and as quickly as the thought is there, Inside Clare shuts it down. And, unvented, the hysteria intensifies to more anger and the need to escape.

Clare makes a dash to the door then stops. She turns and imitates David in the shower. 'Fuckfuckfuckfuckfuckfuck-caaaaaark!'

He stares at her and laughs.

Jas comes into the bathroom and stands behind her mother. She is about to say something then pokes her in the back. 'Good work on the bandages, Mum.'

'He wouldn't sit still!'

'Yeah, that old man thing.' David chuckles.

Jas chooses to ignore what they are laughing about and holds up two golden tins of Rawleigh's ointment. 'I think these are for your friend Neil,' she says.

David is puzzled.

'They're presents for his babies. His twins. Look.' And she opens the tins to show him the beautiful bird feathers stored inside – from drongos, azure kingfishers, satin bowerbirds and exotic technicolour parrots, as well as kestrel down and the crests of various finches.

'Neil has kids?' says Clare.

David hesitates and says simply, 'Everyone has their secrets.'

'Well, he obviously told Pop,' says Jas. 'He wrote a little note in one of them, see,' she says quietly. 'They were a present. *Dear Neil*,' she reads. '*Two tins of magic, like the one I gave you when you would pick on the farm for my father – for your little ones. I am so very happy for you and your lovely wife. Yours, Tony.* That's my pop.'

'I don't think Neil actually wants people to know about his – situation, just at the moment,' says David.

'Well, my pop wanted him to have these. They're so beautiful.' Jas sounds like a little girl.

'They are,' says David, and he explains how rare and lovely some of the birds are.

Jas turns to Clare. 'Mum! This is why you can't just throw everything out!' She holds up two fingers. 'Twice, Mum, twice.'

Clare nods.

'Are we going now? Birding?' asks her daughter.

Clare looks down to David, still perched on the edge of the bath.

David looks up at Clare.

CHAPTER NINETEEN

They go first to the northern mudflats, driving in Tony Cirillo's car. Some other birders are there already, darting about, looking efficient, spotting and marking birds down quickly.

'They look very busy,' says Clare.

David nods. 'It's a twitching day – you have a set time to see how many different birds you can spot. It's a competition, basically.'

'Like bird "spotto"?' asks Jas.

'Basically.' David waves in reply to a curt nod of greeting from an older birder as the group he is part of bustle up a disused boat ramp and into their wagon.

David stares after them for a while. Twitching day. People must have decided that the PPMG has moved on, that there's no point concentrating on finding the one bird. Might as well make a day of it.

Suddenly, he hears Jas laughing, her binoculars trained on an osprey. She has been following the bird circling above them.

He looks at her, remembering doing much the same when he was younger – looking at the one bird for what seemed like an age, trying to understand its markings and then delighting in almost every move the bird made, every inclination of its head and adjustment of its wings.

'You thought it was funny,' says Clare, approaching him.

David looks at her. He tilts his head and his stretched face has a quizzical look. Clare repeats the question, not louder but clearer with more deliberate enunciation.

With his head in the preferred listening position he can hear her relatively clearly. He taps his ear and says, 'This way is all good. But thank you.'

Clare nods.

'What did I think was funny?'

'Before, in the bathroom.'

David mouths an 'Oh'.

'You think it's funny when people yell at you. Are you that disengaged from the world?'

'Yelling doesn't bother me. I grew up with people yelling. No, apparently I sulk when I'm wrong. When it's pointed out to me that I'm irrefutably wrong. That can take me a couple of days to get over.'

'Like when Don told you you had the wrong bird?'

David winces slightly, remembering when Don had corrected him last night about not having spotted the pale pygmy magpie goose. 'That was sulking? Well, I did have a point; I mean he didn't have to put it like that.'

'And you know it. I mean, you've analysed yourself.'

'No. I have four older sisters – it was like I had five mothers. We workshopped everything. They still do when we get together. They're all very kind and tell me the reason I can't commit is that I'm in the closet. Or I'm a spoilt little bastard who has no consideration for women's body clocks. That the birdwatching is just an escape, that I haven't grown up. That I'm going to be a sad old man with a vacuous plastic teenager on my arms.'

'Do they have kids?'

'Thousands. Two of their kids have kids. Christmas is a nightmare. It costs me a fortune to maintain my favourite-uncle status. And on our side, I'm their only one.'

'Do you have kids?'

David is startled. 'Me?' He cocks his head to one side.

'I mean, do you want kids? *Did* you want kids?'

David shrugs. 'I don't really think about it,' he says. 'My sisters do all that for me. I'm too selfish. Too childish. Apparently my life will be meaningless until I have a kid. That's a theory that's tested at family get-togethers.' He puts his binoculars to his eyes and takes in some large-billed gerygones moving in the middle of the mangroves. 'I don't know how their poor brains even work after a day with their kids, never mind how they have time to find meaning in it.

'My youngest older sister – she has two. Not as old as Jas, but getting there. And she confided in me that her worst current fear is that soon they'll be staying up as late as her and she won't even have the joy of tucking them up anymore, of pouring herself a butterscotch schnapps and putting on *30 Rock* or whatever it is people watch these days.'

Clare listens to his story and laughs. David smiles at her.

Jas squeals in delight as the osprey suddenly dives, grasps at something just on the surface of the water and then slowly climbs back into the sky. 'Oh, he missed out!'

Yes, thinks David, the osprey won't be the only one. He knows that he isn't going to hurry anybody along today in trying to find the bird. He probably knew that even as he said to them last night that they could look for the bird together. Somehow he doesn't mind.

Jas turns around to look at him and frowns like her mother. 'What's the point of a twitch if you really want to know about birds?'

David looks at a mob of common sandpipers skating along the water's edge. 'It can be about both.'

'But all you're doing is rushing in, getting a tick and then rushing on. Even if the bird was doing something awesome you wouldn't stop.'

'But you have to know your birds to be able to twitch. You can do both.' He points to the sandpiper. 'They're common sandpipers but down in Victoria they're called *un*common sandpipers. Somebody told me that on a twitching day when I wasn't much older than you are now.'

Jas frowns again, unable to imagine David ever being young like her.

David thinks for a minute. 'It's just like . . . a concert. The enjoyment isn't really about the concert, it's about what the music does for you every day.'

He hears Clare speak and turns to her.

'But the concert is about the music,' she says, 'because it's about hearing your music and the audience becoming part of the music; it's the music at its highest point.'

'Well, I reckon music isn't the right word then,' says Jas as she trains her glasses on the osprey again. 'It's like saying you enjoy all sorts of food and trying to find out how it's made and about the country that food comes from but you also like going in a how-many-hot-dogs-can-you-eat-in-five-minutes competition.'

David laughs. Clare smiles. And so does her daughter.

David's phone vibrates in his pocket with two messages. One is from Don Barrellon, saying that his group have seen lots of birds but no PPMG: *Our special seems to have flown.*

The second one is from Neil telling him he can pick him up from the Cirillos' and take him back to the service station to collect the cream-bun submarine. It ended with: *Any luck?*

David texts back a brief message, his dexterity impressing Jas.

'Good news?' asks Clare.

'Not really.' David jiggles the phone in his hand. 'I don't hear calls very well anymore so I have to send messages. It's okay if I've got earphones but they're like sunglasses – I always lose them. People have to leave messages on my answer machine at home for me to be able to get things straight these days.'

'Can't you get a hearing aid?'

'They make sound different, not just louder.'

The three of them stand quietly, watching the mudflats, and David feels Clare – very gently – take hold of his hand for a few moments.

'I'm sorry,' she says.

He looks towards her. And her face is open and lovely for a few moments before she bursts into laughter. She tries to stop but it's beyond her. 'I'm sorry, it's your eye.' She makes a face to show him.

'Mum,' Jas scolds, 'it's not like that – more like this.' And she contorts her face.

David feels very happy. Then his phone vibrates again. It's a message from Neil. *Try Wonga? And then maybe the Mossman.*

By the time they reach Wonga the weather has begun to close in again. As they watch, a great-billed heron somehow, almost impossibly, manages to lift itself off the ground and half-glide, half-fly to a clearing not far from where they stand. It settles with grace, like a cross between some prehistoric creature and a ballet dancer. Sand plovers group together, then rise and circle the beach until they come in to land in almost the same spot as where they took off.

Dark clouds signal that rain is on the way, confirmed by a poetic text message from Don: *Southern beaches, pissing down, just smoking in the wet.*

'Well, that's a keeper,' David says, showing it to Clare. 'Maybe it'll even make it as a haiku Picnic read.'

She smiles. 'At least we can get a coffee.' And she points to a kiosk at the main end of the beach.

'And a sausage roll – the kiosk has really good sausage rolls,' says Jas.

'The mythical "good sausage roll",' says David. 'Might as well go and see – I've got a better chance of seeing that than the PPMG.'

Jas walks up to David and punches him softly in the arm. 'The sausie rolls are good. And if your goose is migratory, you can always come back, can't you?'

David shrugs his shoulders. 'Guess so.'

Clare doesn't know what to say, but a part of her thinks that would be good. 'Why is your goose so special?' she asks.

'Well, it's very hard to find!'

'Obviously.' Jas rolls her eyes.

'Obviously, but why is it special?' David thinks. 'Well, it's a very subtle bird. Delicate, yet it flies thousands of kilometres. And, I know I've only seen it in pictures, but there's just something about it. Lovely eyes. And it sings.'

'Gooses honk.'

'Geese,' corrects Clare. Jas makes a face.

'Well, this one sings. Sort of. Not *tra la la tweet tweet*, but it's a song – a series of high and low notes. I've listened to recordings.'

As they reach the kiosk David turns to Clare. 'Maybe I could come back? To see my singing goose.'

Clare stares at him then walks ahead into the kiosk.

Inside are a couple of fishermen who have evidently called it a day and a foursome who can only be birders. They spot David and give a nod of acknowledgement, which is returned by David and then Jas. 'Weather's done us, I'd say,' says one of the older birders.

David doesn't quite hear but can guess from the man's gesture to the darkening sky what he is talking about, so he nods. 'Not much you can do,' he agrees.

'Yeah, not much,' says the man. 'Get a sausage roll into you.'

David still can't hear the man but sees him steal a quick second look at his face, and says, 'I had an argument with the branch of a tree this morning.'

'You'd better have two, then,' says the old birder.

David goes to the counter while Jas and Clare sit down near the birders.

Jas thinks it's funny but Clare isn't listening. She's recognised a woman who is making her way back from the bathrooms to the table where the birders sit.

Clare looks away, suddenly feeling awkward, shy and embarrassed for no other reason than that she is Clare, someone who always tries to make herself as invisible as possible. Then the woman notices her, hesitates, as if understanding Clare's state, but thinks better of it and decides to come over.

'Hello, Clare.'

Despite herself Clare smiles. 'Hello, Mrs Boscombe.'

'Oh, it's Shirley.' The woman turns to Jas. 'She used to swim in our pool, your mother, and you couldn't get her out of it to save your life.'

'Shirley is an old friend of your pop's,' Clare says.

Jas remembers the old lady from her grandfather's funeral. She had said over and over again on the day, 'Tony, what a gent.'

Mrs Boscombe nods now. 'Yes, your pop, what a gent. Knew him from little school.'

'You went to school with Pop?'

'Well, little school. Tony went off to boarding school after that. He was very bright, your pop.'

'Do you remember a girl called Penny?' asks Jas.

Mrs Boscombe is slightly taken aback. She considers. 'Penny?' She looks down at the teenage girl. 'Why yes, Penny MacDonald. Penelope. Pretty Penelope.'

'You remember her?'

'Yes, she was a lovely girl. Very lovely. All the boys were sweet on her, if they ever thought about anything else apart from football.'

'What about Pop?'

A stillness descends over Mrs Boscombe for a few moments. She is remembering. 'Your pop? Well, yes, I suppose he spent a lot of time working up the courage to say something to her. Once at big lunch he walked all the way from the top of the playground to where we girls all sat. He walked right up to us and stood there in front of Penny and then he just turned around and ran back.'

Jas stares with wide eyes.

'Poor Penny,' says Mrs Boscombe. 'She died, you know, not long after that – in the holidays; drowned in a dam.'

Nobody says anything.

'Why are you asking after Penny MacDonald, love?'

Jas looks at Clare.

Clare manages, 'Oh, we just found some old school stuff of Dad's when we were cleaning up.'

Mrs Boscombe nods. 'Long time ago now. Very sad. But your father, he was such a gent.' And before she says her goodbyes, Mrs Boscombe looks outside. 'Shame about the weather.'

Ignoring her, Jas glares at her mother, quoting her throwaway comment from the previous day. 'It's just old stuff.' And gets up and runs outside.

Clare tries to call after her, but thinks she might cry. Oh Christ, who is she kidding? She *is* going to cry.

David returns with the food, not quite sure what is

going on. He looks after Jas, then back to Clare, to see her eyes brimming with tears.

She stands up, too. 'I'm going to wait in the car.'

She leaves the kiosk and David is left with three sausage rolls and coffees. He tosses up between going after Clare or Jas, and decides to take a punt on the teenager.

He finds her sitting on the rocks not far from the point, her head resting on her knees.

'You forgot your sausage roll,' he says, handing it to her. She doesn't reply.

A cormorant is inexplicably hanging its wings out to dry.

'Good luck with that, old mate,' says David to the bird. 'It's really going to pour in a minute.'

A kookaburra lands in a tree not far from the rocks, stays a few seconds, casting an eye down on them, and then powers off and up to the trees behind.

'Kookaburras. I always think they fly like an F-111.'

'What?' asks Jas, irritated.

'It was an air force plane that was around when I started birdwatching, I guess. You'd always see them on Australia Day doing fly-pasts. They did this thing called a dump-and-burn – great flames would pour out of the tail. Pretty cool.' David can see that Jas isn't interested.

'When did you start?' she asks him.

'When I was about twelve. There was an old lady who lived near us and Mum used to make me run errands for her. Well, Mum did the errands but she was too shy to actually go in and offer so she used to make me.'

'Really?' Jas is amazed.

'Anyway, it got so this old lady wasn't going out much, and one day she gave me her binoculars and a bird book. I think she thought the end was coming for her. She didn't have any children.'

'The "captain's binoculars"?'

David looks at her. 'How did you know about those?'

'My pop called them that; he left a note about you.' She pauses, then asks, 'What happened to her husband?'

David looks at her. Not strange questions, but not ones he would expect, either. 'He was killed in the war, not long after they were married.'

'Oh.' Jas's eyes suddenly moisten with tears.

David, floundering now, carries on talking. 'She had a dog.'

'What kind?'

'Not sure, very cute and faithful. Followed her everywhere. Whenever she sat down she, the dog, would manage to get on her lap. If I went over and Mrs Ellis was making a cup of tea for us, Angel would sit on my lap. It had to be a lap, or the couch. I don't think that dog's bottom ever touched the floor. Mrs Ellis would sometimes tell me to push her off, but Angel would just turn into this limp dead weight, on purpose, and you couldn't move her. It was like she controlled gravity.' David hasn't thought about Mrs Ellis and Angel for ages.

'Did she give you her house when she died?'

'No. She had a niece, I think.'

'Didn't the niece like birdwatching?'

'I don't suppose so.'

'How did she know she was going to die and not need them anymore?'

David thinks, then half-smiles at the memory. 'We lived near Blackburn Lake in Melbourne; I think she looked at birds there a bit. That's where I started going. But her great love was seabirds. She loved them. Some seabirds never land.'

'Never?'

'Hardly. Every year she went on a trip, on a boat. It took five or six months.'

'What about Angel?' Jas asks.

'She took Angel. I think the crew let Mrs Ellis sneak her aboard. She went on the same boat every year. It was a cargo ship, one of those really big ones. They sometimes have cabins for passengers. Mrs Ellis told me she hated all the fuss and noise on the cruise ships. She used to just like to sit and watch the water go past, looking through her binoculars at the birds. She saw giant albatrosses, storm petrels . . .'

'Have you seen all those birds?'

'No. I'm just interested in Australia really. So I've seen the ones that come into Australian waters, but not all of them do. I've caught a few little boats, just to go offshore. I love boats, but I'm not sure about the sleeping-onboard idea.

'But Mrs Ellis used to tell me that she wanted to die at sea. She wanted to be sitting out of the wind, having been watching a seabird surfing the thermals, only inches from the water. Then she would feel sleepy, have a little nap, which would become a longer nap, then the longest nap.'

Jas shakes her head dismissively. 'People always want it to happen like that. So why didn't she?'

'It was Angel, actually. She stuck so close by Mrs Ellis that one day the old lady tripped over the dog and fell and broke her hip. My mum was in our backyard and heard her calling. Mum phoned the ambulance. We looked after Angel until Mrs Ellis came home. But she never walked properly after that – she had a Zimmer frame.'

Jas gives him a questioning look.

'One of those things you push, but you can lean on them, too – they help you to sit.'

'I love them! I wanted one to take to school. My bag's so heavy, and you never get a seat when you're a schoolkid – because you're "young and fit".'

'You *are* young and fit,' says David.

Jas shrugs. 'So she could have still gone on a boat, then?'

David shakes his head. 'No. She couldn't get her medical certificate or whatever. Mum was helping her a lot so she knew all about it. She said it was the most romantic thing. Mrs Ellis tried to forge a certificate and the captain accepted it, but the company contacted Mrs Ellis's doctor and he said she shouldn't travel; there was a good chance she would die at sea. Even though that's exactly what she wanted. So the company cancelled her booking. Mrs Ellis was really pissed off. Oh – sorry, upset, but there was nothing she could do.' David is silent for a moment.

'So she gave you her binoculars?'

'Not straight away. When the boat was due to dock in Melbourne, Mum offered to drive Mrs Ellis down to the port to see the crew – say goodbye and all. But she didn't want to go. Then the next day the captain came to see her! I only saw him when he was leaving. He was this tall old man in a full uniform, you know, with the stripes and gold buttons.'

'And the hat?' asks Jas, sketching one above her head.

'Yep, the works. Mum was there, so she told us all about it afterwards. The captain was German, and in all the time she'd spent on that boat Mrs Ellis had assumed he hadn't understood her, but when he came to the house, she found out he spoke nearly perfect English.

'Mum said Mrs Ellis was really shocked, and a bit upset, but the captain said he knew Mrs Ellis came on the ship so she didn't have to speak to anyone and liked it that the crew were Filipino and the officers German. Well, I don't think she liked that, or maybe she did; I guess people were more racist in those days. But less unkind and mean.'

'Anyway . . .' Jas prompts him.

'Well, Mum said she left them to talk, and when she went back after four hours they were still drinking tea and catching up on everything. Mrs Ellis told her later that she had always known he was the loveliest, kindest man, and his visit had proved it.'

'Did he take her off on the boat?'

'No. If he lied for her he would lose his captaincy, and she knew how much he loved the sea.'

'Did she wish they'd spoken before? Maybe they would have got married?'

'She told Mum they had had the best relationship in silence and companionship. He promised he would visit her each time he came to port from then on.'

'Did he?'

'He came once more, but she died before he could visit a third time.'

There is a small silence as Jas stares ahead. 'I don't know if that's a sad story or not.'

'I don't think it is. She was eighty-eight.'

'Was she lonely all that time?'

David shrugs.

''Cause she didn't marry?'

'I don't think so. Some people need more of people than others. Some people need to find a space of their own. And you know, people can be lonely even if they're married.'

Jas looks at him. 'Like Mum.'

David thinks for a moment, and wonders at the creature that is a teenage girl.

'My mum is a difficult woman.'

David tries hard not to laugh. 'Well,' he says, 'difficult people are often the best – the most interesting.'

'I know that.' She looks at him fiercely. 'I love her.'

He nods.

'But sometimes she just gives me the absolute irrits.'

'I can see that. Maybe you should just tell her that sometimes, that you love her.'

Jas punches his arm. 'I'm sorry about your singing goose, David Thomas from Melbourne.'

'Thanks.'

Back in the car Clare sits behind the wheel, trying not to cry.

She can see Jas and David running towards her as the rain starts to fall. He has a funny run, she thinks. She remembers him under the shower. A part of her would like to smile but she's also thinking about her father.

The passenger door opens and Jas gets in, while David gets in the back, squeezing his long legs in behind the front seat. Jas closes the car door and puts her seatbelt on.

'I love you, Mum. But sometimes you give me the irrits. And I bet I give them to you, too.' And she leans over and kisses Clare on the cheek. 'David Thomas of Melbourne told me I should tell you that sometimes. I think I will.'

Clare turns around to look at David and he just stares back with his stretched eye.

'Well, there you go,' says Clare.

The rain is very heavy now and Clare asks if David wants to try the Mossman River.

He might have done if he had been alone, but it would have been pointless and he knows it is nearly time for Neil to come and pick him up from Cirillos'. Besides, he realises, he'd rather spend his last hour there.

CHAPTER TWENTY

Picnic is waiting on the verandah next to David's swag and she lopes up to him. David looks at the chest of Picnic reads and decides instead to read the Don Barrellon haiku on his phone. The bird stares at him, nonplussed, making him laugh.

Inside the house, sitting at her father's desk writing, Clare stops when she hears him. His laugh. It sounds like it belongs, a little like the calls of the birds.

Jas comes to the door. 'Mum, look, there's a message on the phone.'

Clare goes over to the old answering machine and presses the playback button. It's from Ollie.

For once there is no background noise from the kids, just her brother's voice. 'Bear, Ollie here. How are you? Just calling to say . . .' There is a pause. 'To say I've been thinking about you staying there in the wild north. It's not such a bad idea; *petite* Clara wants to see crocodiles, you know. And I . . . well, Bear, I love you. I'll ring later.'

Jas stands by the machine. 'Are you staying?'

Clare nods.

Jas walks over and hugs her mother.

'Now, did you bring those things?'

Jas nods. 'Should we do it?'

Clare looks at her daughter; she seems happy – a bit concerned, but happy to be doing something with her. With her mum. 'Yes, I think we should.'

Jas smiles. 'So do I.'

The rain is just a soft drizzle now, but rumbling thunder in the distance suggests more is on the way. David looks up to the sky, then feels a hand on his arm.

Clare.

'Fancy a last walk to the top orchard? It's got a view overlooking the lagoon.'

David nods.

'Just watch out for the lemons.'

The orchard is on a soft incline and at the top some trees have been felled and set aside for burning, creating a kind of lookout over the tiered lagoons below.

They walk to the top; David takes a photo on his phone.

Clare didn't say anything to him as they walked, and as they stand together she quietly looks at the view.

Sure rain will fall soon, David assumes his head-tilt so he can hear the different bird calls. He sucks in a deep breath as if trying to store every sense of the place he can.

Clare feels very calm. And safe. And even though she isn't sure she wants to say anything she suddenly decides she will. Why not? What a mad few days it's been. It can't get any sillier.

'After Jas's dad and I split up, I was a wreck. It wasn't . . .' She stops and tries to catch David's eye, but with his head tilted that way she decides it'll be easier to carry on staring down at the lagoons instead.

'It wasn't that I loved him that much; I had just never been alone. I had heaps of pride and my self-esteem was wrapped up in being with someone. Nuts, really. I like being alone. I can spend ages alone. I was desperate to have a boyfriend, then a husband, but then I'd want time to myself. Not surprisingly, that didn't always go down well. But after a while it was just Jas and me so I don't suppose I was really alone. And I was fine without . . . a partner.'

She glances at him and the expression on his face hasn't changed. Well, at least he's a good listener for someone who's going deaf, she thinks.

'I'm still gathering up my self-esteem, figuring out what means what to me, but I'm all right. I kind of like figuring it out. I kind of like knowing I'll die and that everything's a cycle and that the world will continue without me.'

David looks at her; her face in this soft light before the storm is gorgeous. Subtle, he thinks. Now there's a word to describe a difficult woman. He thinks then that he has never seen anything so beautiful.

'I used to think when I was young,' says Clare, 'that the world was only here when I was here. Not in a world-revolving-around-me kind of way – more like thinking everyone's pretending – and as soon as I'm somewhere else they'll all sit around with a beer and have a good laugh about how I keep falling for it.' She pauses. 'That makes me seem like I have a massive ego, doesn't it?' She looks at him again as she finishes.

'No, not at all. Never in a million years, Clare.'

He moves closer. She turns to him.

And then they hear it.

David first, of all people.

Three notes at first; soft, like a gentle flute.

They look at each other. Clare can hear it, too.

'Is that your bird?'

He doesn't move. It sings again. From the direction of the sound, the bird might be below them, in one of the lagoons, or near them, at the water's edge.

If he turned he could see. But instead he looks at Clare.

Beautiful. He feels goosebumps.

Clare can see, in the lagoon below, a bird. Softly coloured and gentle. It glides to the edge of the water. It looks up, ruffling its feathers.

'It's your bird,' she says quietly.

'I know,' says David. He is watching her, he can't turn away.

'Look down there,' she coaxes him.

'No.'

And they kiss.

When they look again, the lagoon is empty of birds. Clare turns and walks quickly back to the house, David following in silence.

David had tried to say sorry, but Clare had kissed him back; it wasn't just him kissing her.

He goes to say something, but as they reach the verandah, they see Neil is already there, waiting.

'Better go before it buckets down,' he calls.

David nods and grabs his swag and backpack, and Neil sees the bandage on his head.

'Now you *are* looking good, David. How did you go?'

'I have no bloody idea.'

Neil is about to question him further when Jas comes out through the front door holding two golden tins.

'Murph,' says Clare steadily, 'these are from your dear friend Antonio Cirillo. A gift to your children.'

Neil stares in shock and looks at David.

'He didn't tell,' says Clare. 'Jas found them. A gift for your twins.'

Neil takes the tins; noticing their lightness, he realises what's in them. He's still watchful – like a magpie. His lip trembles a little.

Clare walks up to him. 'And this is from Jas and me.' She hands him an envelope containing the card she had just written at the desk. 'It's an invitation for you and Lily – and her mother – to come here, any time, whenever you want.'

Neil looks up. 'You staying?' he asks.

Jas almost shouts, 'We sure are!'

Neil nods. 'Well, good to hear, Bear; we'll take you up on that.'

David stands at the Land Rover. Waiting. Neil gets in and starts the engine, when David suddenly remembers something.

'Wait a tick!' He turns away from the car and reaches into his pocket.

Clare sees him coming; she remains calm and holds out her hand to shake goodbye.

David takes it, and places a feather in her palm. A wing feather of the azure kingfisher.

'For you,' he says. And with that he leaves.

Melbourne. Not wild tonight, but familiar and safe and home. He makes his way into his flat, remembers its smell. His smell, he supposes. It feels like he's been away for weeks, rather than three days.

He thinks of Mr Peachy. Dear old Mr Peachy. He thinks about him for a time as he sits. Alone.

Then he sees that the answering machine is blinking. It's probably work. He presses play. And he hears the sounds of the north, and a voice. The voice of a difficult woman.

'Hello. Grumpy girl seeks gorgeous bird nerd to share a verandah and Picnic reads. And wants to find his singing goose.'

'Hot Diggity,' he says to himself.

And he reaches for the phone.

ACKNOWLEDGEMENTS

I would like to acknowledge in no particular order but with equal thanks, Kate Ballard, Anna Egelstaff, Jessica Luca and everyone at Hachette; Emma Kelly, Clara Finlay, Samantha Collins and Simon Paterson; and especially Clem and Stella McInnes.

INTRODUCING
HOLIDAYS
BY
WILLIAM MCINNES
(ABRIDGED)

I once had a part-time clerical job in a public service department that dealt with family allowance forms. We were given the rather unfortunate title of FA Monitors, or Sweet FA monitors, as one man, George, insisted on saying when he answered the phone.

'That's all we do, sweet FA,' he said with a smile.

I couldn't really disagree, we all seemed to simply sift through our forms, stamp a section and file them away in large yellow envelopes that then disappeared down to a room in the basement. Although the work was dull, the sweet FA monitors were an interesting group of people.

George, a bearded man with round rimless spectacles, was a Nudgee College old boy who looked like an illustration from an 1890s Anarchist International handbook, which was apt as he happened to be a member of the International Socialists.

There was a Polish vet who was waiting for her academic credentials to be recognised in Australia, and a large woman who put sugar on her hot chips because she was diabetic. I only found this out when I asked her why she was pouring the contents of a large plastic Saxby salt container over her fried food.

'Sugar,' she corrected.

'Sorry?' I said.

'It's sugar.'

'Sugar.' I nodded.

'Because I am diabetic,' she said.

I didn't know if that made any sense but I nodded again.

'Why do you put the sugar in the salt container?'

'Because it makes me feel normal.'

'Nobody puts that much salt on their chips,' George said.

'It's sugar.'

'You are normal,' a woman who looked like Oscar Wilde said.

'Am I?' said the sugar salt sprinkler.

'You are to me,' said Oscar Wilde. 'Very normal.'

'Thank you.' And she sprinkled more sugar from the salt container.

One of the Sweet FA monitors was a strange man who hardly said anything but had a habit of whistling 'Two Little Girls in Blue' as he walked through the office. He was a small, emaciated man with lank hair and a drooping moustache who reminded me of Mathew Brady photographs from the American Civil War. He floated through the halls like the spectre of one of General Grant's whiskey-swilling inner circle.

Our supervisor, Lew, was anything but a spectre, a stocky man with a surfer's bleached shoulder-length hair, tight pants and short-sleeved shirts always adorned by a broad tie.

He had rather bad skin and would walk about with a nod, dipping a finger in his mouth and then daubing a bit of spittle on something he was picking at on his arm.

Once a day, the world's most violent tea lady would storm about and bully people into buying something from her trolley, all the while dispensing personal advice and character assessments.

'You want to put a bit more weight on, mate,' she said to the civil war spectre.

'Still picking at yourself, Lew? Feed your hobby with some choccy! Zit fertiliser.'

Lew smiled as he bought some chocolate and picked at himself.

The section manager was a man called Phil, with a Dennis Lillee moustache and neatly combed, tortured hair. He was either constantly on the phone or going through calculations in a low mutter at his desk.

It was only when I was moved closer to Phil's desk and overheard his conversations that I started to understand how far and wide the FA monitors' work spread.

Phil spoke like a radio presenter from 4IP during Rocktober, smooth and certain, save for the fact he couldn't pronounce his r's.

'Okay, Slacks Cweek are all in and the Northern suburbs are done. Gweat.' A few phone calls later, 'Amewica, West Coast and Wocky Mountains?' and then, 'What about a Bawewier Weef for the short term?'

From Slacks Creek to the Rocky Mountains to the Great Barrier Reef.

I was never sure what any of us was supposed to be doing but, in between creating a ball made of discarded rubber bands the size of a soccer ball and stamping my forms, the most exotic suburb that I saw mentioned on any form was Lota, down past Wynnum but nowhere near the Rockies.

On my final day, during a tea trolley round, Phil enlightened me about what we sweet FAs did.

I asked the tea lady for a Cherry Ripe, Lew picked at himself, the Polish vet bought an apple, and the sugar salt sprinkler asked for a couple of salt sachets to mix up her chip seasoning. Oscar Wilde sat smiling. The tea lady asked me how my last day was going.

'No last-day shivers, Stretch? Not worried where you're going?'

I told her I was okay and that I never really knew what it was we were doing there anyway.

There was a silence.

Eventually Rock-tober Phil filled it.

'Intwesting, Willyum. Intwesting. Not just about forms and filing what we do here, you know. Just a means to an end. We pwovide a service, twue, but it's a means to an end.'

'To what?'

Rock-tober Phil laughed. 'To what? I'm fairly incwedulous, Will. To *what*?'

It was like I was some poor sod who had missed a basic truth about the purpose of work.

There was a gurgle behind me from the civil war spectre. I looked at him and to my astonishment realised he was talking.

'Holidays,' he said, smiling.

Everyone else around the trolley nodded. 'Holidays.' And they laughed.

I understood.

Holidays.

'How you measure your good times,' said Phil. He winked at the tea lady. 'Will's Chewee Wipe is on me.'

It was as if a life could have its happiness measured in holidays.

Work and toil might be a part of life, even at the Sweet FAs, but it is the golden moments of a holiday – with your children, your partner, your loved ones and friends – that you remember. They can determine your happiness.

I like to think all the Sweet FAs had holidays they remembered.

Because for them, like so many Australians, a holiday is a special time that you have either worked hard and long for, or come by with a stroke of good luck, or simply look forward to achieving. It's a reward for lasting through work or school, or some period of life, to reach that state of nirvana of being on holiday.

But first, before that blissful state, you have to understand what a holiday actually is and then perhaps you'll understand what it means to you.

•

The first holiday I can remember going on was with my mother and brother and three sisters. We waved goodbye to the dog, a rusty red kelpie cross called Michael, and my father, who was called Colin by my mother and Col by every other person we or he ever came into contact with.

Col and Michael stood at the gate as we rolled away on the Green Hornibrook Bus that would take us across a long and bumpy bridge to Sandgate railway station. We were to board a train to South Brisbane, then another to

Sydney and another to Camden, west of Sydney, where we were to stay with my aunt on a dairy farm.

Train travel meant going to Brisbane. I was only six but I knew that much. That meant the Brisbane Show or a movie or the museum, with the German tank and the dinosaur outside. Or lunch in the Coles cafeteria with the ladies in the white uniforms and the crumbed sausages with yellow runny cheese in the middle, and roast chicken and gravy. Gravy without lumps, almost unimaginable.

At home, Mum would have a crack at gravy and my father would say, 'You've mined the harbour again, 'Ris!' as he happily sifted through the little balls of flour in Mum's gravy.

'Well, try cooking for you lot,' my mother would say.

A holiday could also mean plastic cups of lime jelly with cream and a chocolate frog.

But this train trip holiday was special because we were not only going to Brisbane but past Brisbane. I had no concept of what was past Brisbane but my eldest sister, Laurie, explained the holiday to me.

'We're going on a trip. A long trip. A long, *long* train trip.'

She might as well have said that we were sailing round the world but she assured me that it would be worth it.

At Sandgate railway station, the holiday began.

We waited, teetering on the edge of the platform to watch the approaching train until we were grabbed and hauled back by our mother's hand.

After the train arrived, we scrambled on board and peered out the windows. From the top carriage, we looked over the backyards that slowly rolled past and counted the number of above-ground pools.

It was exciting. Especially as my sister Corby had told me that we might see proper pools. In-ground pools. I looked into backyards filled with fibro sheds, banana trees, cars on blocks and caravans.

I spotted an old dog barking and an old woman with a cane yelling at an old man who looked away and waved his arm at her.

'Are they on holiday?' I asked.

My mother laughed.

I saw a little girl standing still beneath a Hills Hoist holding on to a towel and staring out at the train.

'She's not going on a holiday,' said one of my sisters.

I waved as we chugged slowly past the girl. She kept holding the towel, but with her other hand she gave a slight, slow little wave.

But I never saw any proper pools.

When we arrived at far distant South Brisbane I was stunned to discover that we weren't in Camden yet.

I still wasn't clear on what a holiday was, despite my mother explaining to me earlier in the week that a holiday is a bit of time where you do lovely things that you never get the chance to ever really do.

Like?

My sister Corby went to the Oxford Dictionary, which I knew would explain what a holiday was, for there was no word that it did not explain. The worth of this book was proven when my elder sisters would take great delight in telling me the definition of fart – 'an emission of pungent gas/wind from between the legs'.

It was, I think, the funniest thing anyone had ever read out from a book, barring the time my father had attempted to read a story to me in bed without his glasses. He couldn't see a word of the book about the three little pigs so he decided to make it up.

Dad stood up for the wolf because 'Old Wolfie' did what wolves were supposed to do and never complained. Wolfie seemed to take his fate like a man, or, as my father put it, 'Copped it fair on the chin without a whimper,' even when he fell in the pot of boiling water. The pigs, on the other hand, were all soft, podgy and had tickets on themselves.

Particularly the pig from the house of bricks. For some reason Dad had it in for this pig. 'Smug, fat little sod, that's what he is,' muttered my dad.

'Where'd he get the money to pay for that? Eh?'

My father had it sorted; Old Wolfie hadn't fallen into a boiling pot of water but had jumped into a bath. The fat little pig who hid in his house of bricks hadn't given Wolfie any soap for the bath and so, quite reasonably, Wolfie jumped out of the water, gobbled up the pigs and then opened up a pub that sold sarsaparilla.

The three little pigs would forever be coloured by that evening's night-night read.

But when it came to holidays, the Oxford Dictionary gave only a rather dry and befuddling definition. Maybe if my father could have read it without his glasses it might have been better, but he was out working.

I had to make do with this: 'holiday – an extended period of leisure and recreation, especially one spent away from home or travelling'.

Leisure and recreation were explained as things like reading, running, swimming, playing, relaxing and watching telly.

These were things I seemed to spend most of my time doing. So I still didn't quite know what a holiday was because, really, all my life had seemed a holiday.

I knew this thing called a holiday was different though, because we all got dressed up for it.

I cried because my mother had the final say on what was suitable attire and I couldn't wear an ice cream bucket as a helmet.

And because I wasn't allowed to wear a t-shirt.

The button-up shirt was what my mother wanted; I had to look like I belonged to someone. It was special. We were going on holidays.

So for the next sixteen hours on the train we wore our best clothes.

'It's important to let people know that we've made an effort,' Mum said.

A holiday was also important enough to pack food for. Not as in food for a picnic or day trip but a bag with platoons of sweet corn sandwiches, a battalion of boiled eggs, and tubes of condensed milk with a polar bear on the side.

We ate on the train and bits of corn spilled here and there, and rolled around the carriages. My brother, Vaughan, put some corn in his mouth and smiled as if he had only a few yellow old teeth in his head. 'Kissy on ya yips! Kissy on ya yips,' he said to me.

I squirmed and wriggled, whined and lost the contents of my sweet corn sandwich over my good shorts.

Vaughan laughed and puckered his lips, and his yellow sweet corn teeth spilled out onto the floor.

My mother shook me and gave Vaughan a flick. 'Stupid boys.'

I wondered if this was her leisure time, sitting with her tribe of unruly children. Even though it must have been like wrangling cats in a bag, she looked sort of happy. It was a holiday.

A holiday in a train carriage for hours and hours as we trundled past small towns. Our copious boiled eggs ensured that the carriage was filled with a fair amount of pungent gas being emitted from between the legs. Thanks to the Oxford Dictionary.

Why my father didn't come on the holiday was a mystery to me.

'We all can't have fun on holiday, you know, somebody has to keep things going.' Those were my father's last words as he eagerly waved us goodbye.

Transporting five children interstate might have been my father's idea of fun but my mother never said anything. Eventually the train, and us, got to her.

The train was such an important part of that first holiday because it was another world in itself.

The dark, winding carriages and compartments that rolled to and fro, and the way we were gently rocked as we walked the aisles to the little shop that sold bits and pieces of chewy and chocolate and little bags of crisps. Or we'd walk to the drinking basin that pulled down from the wall with two glasses either side of a flat glass beaker.

We'd sway past the odd paintings on the walls. A long tall glass of beer advertising Reschs; Namatjira landscapes, one with an Aborigine standing with the sole of one foot stuck flat to the knee and shin of his other leg. A spear held upright.

For hours we kids roamed up and down the train and my mother never said anything until the toilet. She had managed her wild tribe of children and the sweet corn and eggs but it was the toilet that did it, and me.

The toilet was a tight cold cupboard where barely one person could fit in to do their business. But the size was not the toilet's true terror.

'Just wait till you go to the toilet and do number twos.' My brother smiled.

I just stared.

He smiled.

'Mum, what's wrong with the toily?'

My mother said there was nothing wrong with the toilet.

'Just you wait,' said my brother.

I had to go sooner or later and when I did – wanting to make sure that there wasn't substance to my brother's teasing – I whined until one of my sisters came with me.

Corby and I rocked towards the toilet. When we passed the painting of the Aborigine with his spear, Corby told me, 'I'm not going in there with you, you know. You're a big boy now.'

She assured me she'd be just outside. I opened the stiff, hard little door and closed it. I stood in the cupboard and stared down at the stainless-steel toilet.

It didn't look threatening at all.

Just another toilet. Vaughan was just teasing.

'Hurry up,' said Corby from outside the door.

I got down to business and lifted the lid. And screamed.

Below the toilet was a blur, like someone flicking through the pages of a picture book quickly. The strange funnel-shaped bowl was like a crazy kaleidoscope giving a distorting view of what whizzed by below. I suddenly saw the sleepers of the train tracks sliding past like giant piano keys.

And the noise was like some great roaring monster. I wasn't going to use that toilet. There wasn't any need.

I did what I had to do in my pants. I knew one thing – I didn't want to do a number two down the cupboard's roaring hole.

My mother took charge of the trips to the toilet after that. She would hold me, squirming in her great strong arms, yelling at me, 'Stop wriggling about! Just sit there and do it.'

She managed to conquer the toilet in the end but it was only a matter of time before the holiday train got the upper hand.

Some new passengers were on the train. Two of them were a young Italian couple. He was happy and eager. She was young and very pretty and wore beautiful soft clothes.

She sat not far from us and smiled as I passed by with my mother. After a while she looked towards my mother, who quite frankly and justifiably, probably felt like she was having anything but a time of recreation and leisure.

'All yours,' said the young woman in an Italian accent and she nodded to us five children as we draped ourselves over and around the seats.

'All of them,' said my mum.

The young man laughed and put his arm around the young woman and pulled gently at the skin beneath her soft clothes.

'Some day we will have children,' he said.

Her soft eyes looked at all of us. She didn't smile and she looked down.

The couple got off just before Sydney and as the young woman readied herself to leave she gave us children and Mum some sugar-covered almonds and pieces of nougat wedding cake.

As they walked along the platform, we all waved to them and they smiled back.

My mother said softly as the young woman walked away, 'Poor little thing.'

I had another unsuccessful trip to the roaring cupboard before we changed trains at Sydney for Campbelltown and I still had wet pants as my exhausted mother dragged us to our new train.

'It can only get better, it can only get better,' she whispered like a prayer and then she began to laugh.

Above us at Central Station a huge flock of flying foxes rolled over the sky. We all stared.

'Just look at that,' said my mother, 'that's the way to travel.'

That train to Campbelltown happened to be a steam train and the smell of the smoke was strong.

I said incessantly that I wanted to see the smoke and my mother finally decided, why not? She held me outside the window in her big strong hands.

'Can you see the smoke?' she yelled.

I tried to say yes but got a mouthful of soot and ash. So I nodded.

That was when my first holiday really began, for it's not every day a mother holds her youngest out a train window. In my mother's hands, and hearing her laugh, I knew that this holiday, this train holiday, was fun.

●

The journey home was something I have no discernible memory of, save for coming back from Sandgate station on the green bus over the long and bumpy bridge, getting off at the stop just a way from our home and walking up the drive, hearing Michael bark.

And my father appearing with a big smile and looking rather tentative as my mother's eyes swept the house to see what he had renovated.

And just before she could yell he covered her in a big hug and said, 'Now 'Ris, it'll look smashing when it's finished.'

A wall or a window or door had disappeared.

I knew my first holiday had ended and a part of me couldn't wait for the next.

From Chapter One of *Holidays* by William McInnes,
published by Hachette Australia